An American Breakfast

Hideo Asano

Published by
Welby Press
Los Angeles

Copyright© 1992 Hideo Asano

Library of Congress Cataloging-in-Publication Data

All rights reserved, including the right to reproduce this
book or portions thereof in any form whatsoever.
For information address: Welby Press,
P.O. Box 862232
Los Angeles, California 90086-2232

ISBN: 0-9635130-0-1

Cover art by Kyoko Hibino

Printed in the United States of America

TO DENNIS, JAMES AND JOE

An American Breakfast

One

The highway, taking Kenji Shimada across country in the fire-engine-red Porshe 914/4 he was delivering to New York, had now become a picture postcard. The amazingly flat landscape of Nebraska, as seen from the interstate throughway, resembled a football field, and was both alive and breathing. The breeze through the open windows carried the powerfully suggestive scent of sweet, growing corn, and nothing, thought Kenji, could be more alive and breathing than that.

Then, without warning, he saw a geyser of black smoke billowing from the engine compartment behind his seat.

Chikusho (damn)!, he swore to himself, remembering the auto delivery representative, who had warned him to check the oil frequently because the oil gauge didn't work properly.

Then he heard a strange noise and quickly turned off the radio to listen closely to the sound of the engine. The noise grew and grew until finally the car began to slow.

Kenji waited a moment and then tried vainly to restart the engine. I may have blown it completely, he said to himself. A bit later he tried again, but to no avail.

He exited the car dejectedly. Then he opened the engine compartment from which smoke billowed. Praying the engine hadn't been permanently damaged, he pulled out the dip stick and was shocked to find the oil level empty. He knew now that his well-planned schedule had been ruined. He closed the hood and angrily kicked the car's tire. Delivering the high-priced sports car to New York seemed a good idea at the time, but the result was becoming disastrous.

He had to reach the nearest town for help. He took his small duffel bag out of the car. Looking up and down the long straight highway, he decided to go east. He stood on the side of the road with his right thumb out, but no cars stopped for him. They all just drove by.

He began walking along the highway. It was very hot, and he had to wipe the perspiration from his face. After walking about an hour, he reached a small town.

He stopped at a gas-station called Jack's where he first rushed to a dust-covered soda machine and bought a 7-Up, which he drank thirstily. Next he approached a red-haired mechanic who was working on a car. He explained his problem.

"First we'll have to tow it. We charge for that."

"I have triple-A." Taking his wallet out of his backpocket he showed the membership card to the mechanic after he put his bag on the hood of a nearby car.

"Good." Then the mechanic gave a second, younger mechanic the location of the broken down car, and told him to tow it up to the station.

"What's the name of this town?" he asked as he took out a big folded map of the U.S. from his bag.

"Grand Island."

He spread the map out on the hood of the car.

"We're right here!" said the mechanic as he pointed with his greasy finger to the map, leaving a black smear. "In the middle of America!"

"Is there a map of this town?"

"Over there," said the man, pointing to a glass window in the office.

The young man walked over and took a look at the oil-stained map of the town and found himself at the point marked: "You are here!"

"By the way, where are you from?"

"Los Angeles."

"Originally, I mean."

"Japan."

Returning, he refolded his map, making sure the clean sides were on the outside, and put it back into his bag.

"Do you think I'll be held responsible since this car broke down on the way to being delivered?"

"I don't know."

"Do you think I'll be reimbursed by the company when I get there?"

"I don't know. Why don't you call them and find out?"

"All right," Kenji said. Again, taking the wallet out of his pocket, he walked to the phone booth and removed the contract paper and then made a call.

"They say it's my responsibility," he later explained despondently to the mechanic.

"That's life."

Two

Thirty minutes later, the Porsche was towed into the station.

"One hell of a beautiful car! What year is it?"

"Seventy-four."

"Let me try to start it," said the short-haired mechanic. The engine was completely dead.

The mechanic opened the engine compartment and examined the dip stick.

"There's no oil!" he said disgustedly.

"Yes."

"When was the last time you checked it?"

"In L.A."

"I hate to tell you this...but you might have blown the engine."

"How much to fix it?" Kenji asked, wiping the sweat from his forehead with the back of his hand.

"I can't tell until I get a good look inside to see the extent of the damage."

"How long will it take?"

"I'm sure it'll take at least a week to get the parts alone, if I can get them at all. Call me tomorrow afternoon. I'll give you an answer then."

"All right."

With his bag in his hand, Kenji left the gas-station and started meandering about town. Where should I stay? he asked himself. In any event, I'll have to call my father in Japan to ask for some money.

A middle-aged woman watering her lawn turned and stared at him as he walked by. A group of boys sitting on the steps of one of the houses stopped talking, nudged one another, and stared at him as if they had never seen an Oriental. Walking in the town he began to feel uncomfortable— even isolated. Nebraska is certainly different from California, he said to himself. Being Oriental never drew any attention there.

He went into a Denny's. Inside, it was cool and clean. Several people, who were sitting at the tables, looked at him intently as he entered. He could feel the weight of their stares. He took a stool at the counter.

"Hi," said a very attractive waitress of about eighteen carrying up a glass of ice water. She had a casually-arranged up-sweep of dark brown hair in which the top fell softly forward, artfully undone.

"May I have a large ice tea?"

"Sure. With lemon?"

"Yes."

He emptied the water with a single gulp and looked at her clean nape as she walked away.

When she returned with the ice tea, he asked, "What's the population of this town?"

"About thirty thousand, I think."

"Small town."

"Oh? Thirty thousand isn't small. Where are you from?"

"L.A."

"What are you doing here? We don't see many foreigners."

"My car broke down on the highway."

"That's too bad."

"Actually, that's not my car. I was delivering it to New York."

"That's really bad. So what are you going to do?"

"I don't know."

"What do you do in Los Angeles?"

"I'm studying at U.S.C."

"How nice!"

"My girlfriend told me that I would get a better understanding of the U.S.A. by driving across it."

"Is she Japanese?"

"No, she is an American just like you. She is Swedish-American."

"What is her name?"

"Inga Svenson."

"That's definitely Swedish. I'm of German descent."

"What is your name?"

"Lisa Snyder," she said, putting out her hand.

"Mine is Kenji Shimada. Nice to meet you."

"What are you studying at U.S.C.?"

"Computer engineering. But I would rather be a writer than an engineer."

"Then why are you studying computer engineering?"

"To please my father. He wants me to be an engineer."

"Sounds like my boyfriend George's father, Henry. He wants George to be a farmer — which George doesn't want to be."

"I see."

"He doesn't even like his son going out with me."

"Why?"

"Because I'm from town. He wants him to marry a farm girl."

"Sounds like my father. My father doesn't like Inga. He wants me to marry a Japanese girl."

"What does Inga do?"

"She also studies computer engineering at U.S.C."

"I wish you both good luck."

"Thanks." With that, Kenji looked at his watch. It was now 5:30 A.M. in Japan. "I have to make a call to my father in Japan to ask for some money. I hate to call to ask just for that."

"But you have no choice."

"You're right." He stood. "Where's the phone?"

"In the corner," she pointed.

He walked to the telephone and dialed the international operator.

As he waited for the various interminable operator's delays, he thought back to the conversation he had just had with the waitress. Her attitudes and mannerisms were quite unlike anything he had encountered in California. In Japan, especially, he couldn't have had that kind of friendly and open conversation with a strange waitress. He enjoyed conversing with her and he once again thought that conversing is quite like playing tennis with certain sounds and expectations. He remembered those painfully lonely days while he was visiting Japan last summer because no one (except with his intimate friends) played the conversation game. The volley he sent hardly ever returned to him. Kenji appreciated that Lisa had been pleasant, and curious, and open, and worried, even though her reactions might have been brought out by his foreignness. Of most importance, he had not been made to feel he was an unwelcome visitor in some bizarre, offbeat world.

Finally, his father, Ichiro Shimada, accepted the call and Kenji was put through.

"*Moshi, moshi.*"

"Dad, this is Kenji. I'm calling from a small town in Nebraska."

"What happened?"

"Probably I have blown the engine of the car I am driving across the country. And I don't have enough money to repair it."

"How much do you need?"

"I don't know yet. I will know tomorrow."

"Is there a Sumitomo or Tokyo bank?"

"I'll ask." Kenji motioned Lisa over and asked her the

question.

"No, I don't think so," she replied. "There's a First National Bank of Omaha nearby and a First National of Kearney down the street."

Kenji told his father, "No, I don't think there are any branches of those banks here."

"Do you have enough for a hotel for a couple days?"

"Yes."

"First of all, I'll send an international money order for 200,000 yen by wire to your hotel. Call your mother when you get a room and give her the name and address of the place."

"I will."

"So how is school going?"

"Very well. I am in the top five percent of my class."

"Excellent."

"Also I've published some short stories in the college magazine."

"Good."

"Inga helped me with my English." I shouldn't have brought that up, Kenji said to himself, recalling his father's distaste of inter-racial relationships.

"Are you still *tsukiatte iru* (going out) with her?" asked Ichiro.

"Yes."

"Listen, she is not of our people and you are not of hers. Don't mix it up!" Ichiro raised his voice.

"Dad, I am more interested in character than race."

"Think about it! If you marry this girl, what will happen to your family? Your children will be *konkettsuji* (half-breeds). *Hazukashii* (shame)! *Hazukashii*! *Kokusai-kekkon* (inter-racial marriage) is an ugly thing! It's not right! It doesn't look good! Whenever I see *baka na Nihon no onna-no-ko tachi* (foolish Japanese girls) who marry white men it disgusts me!"

"Dad, you are are narrow minded."

"You are throwing your future away on an *asonde ru kinpatsu-onna* (blond-haired playgirl)!"

"She is not an *asonde ru onna* (playgirl). She doesn't play around with other men. She loves only me."

"I don't care!"

"She is an intelligent girl. You would like her if you met her."

"No way! I don't want to see her! You are coming back home after you finish school. Alone! I don't want to hear another word about this...American...this intelligent girl!"

"I can't break her heart. You can't just tell me to break off our relationship!"

"Then forget about the 200,000 yen, unless you change your mind!"

"I won't change my mind!"

"Unless you change your mind, I won't send that money, plus don't expect me to send any further tuition!" Ichiro hung up the phone.

Kenji looked at the receiver and then slowly hung it up. He was very disappointed and fast-becoming depressed. Because of Inga his father was disowning him. Here he was, stuck in a small Nebraska town, for who knew how long. Where was he going to get the money to fix the Porsche, and thus get on with his trip to New York?

He was uncertain what to do. He loved Inga and his family with the same intensity and he hated himself because he couldn't think of an acceptable compromise that would please his father. It could only be one of two extreme choices. One, drop Inga and, two, go back to Japan and get a job in a company. This last would make him a company man and he would have to always think like a company man. Next, he would have to marry a Japanese girl to please his father. He would have to stay with that same company and that same woman until the day he died.

He said over and over to himself, I would have a company life, not my own life. I would be a part of a company machine. I know I will have to work until late night almost everyday as I have seen my brother and my father do. I wouldn't ever have any time for myself or for my own family. My future may not hold even one vacation.

If I marry Inga I will loose my family and Japanese culture and will be out of Japanese society. But I wouldn't be a Japanese company man in America. I will have my own life, not company life. I wouldn't be a part of the company machine but instead I'll be my own man. I also can quit the company when I feel I need to and find another job. I will gain individual freedom in the United States.

The more he thought about it, the more it tore at his emotions. He wished that Inga was with him now. He picked up the phone again and made a call to Inga in L.A., but no one answered. Probably working, he thought.

Without Kenji's realizing it, his voice must have risen during the short conversation with his father. Once again, when he returned to the counter, Lisa moved over toward him and said, "The expression on your face can only be called 'bleak.' Bad news from home?"

Kenji hesitated before he replied.

"From all I can figure out," he began, "I may have just adopted a new home...Nebraska."

"What brought all that about?"

Kenji had no choice but to explain what had just transpired.

Lisa replied by exclaiming, "I think that will be your loss and our gain."

"Yes, but please understand. I am not visiting royalty. I am destitute. I must have a job of some sort just to stay alive while the car is being fixed...not to mention being able to pay for the car if all else falls through."

"Maybe you could work on a farm in the meantime."

"I could?"

"You're in farm country. It's corn-growing weather and farmers badly need any farmhand they can get."

"But I don't have any experience."

"I know. I can tell because you're so skinny. If you'd been raised on a farm you'd have a little more meat on you."

"I see."

"If you want, I'll call and ask my boyfriend George."

"All right."

She went to the phone. For the moment Kenji felt good because at least there was a possibility of having a place to stay and to work. She called George.

When she returned, smiling, she said, "He'll be here in thirty minutes to pick you up."

"I can't thank you enough," Kenji smiled. Then he asked. "What kind of crops does George's father grow?"

"It's a dairy farm and he grows corn too."

"Wonderful."

"But he is a very unlucky farmer."

"Why?"

"Last summer there was a hailstorm on his farm which caused him to lose half of his crop. That was his third bad year in a row. Imagine! Three years in a row!"

"Hail? You mean tiny ice chunks like diamonds coming out of the sky?"

"They're this big!" She formed a golf-ball sized circle with her thumb and index finger. "Sometimes they're as big as baseballs."

"In America everything is bigger. I guess even American baseballs are bigger than Japanese baseballs," Kenji joked, overcoming his depression for the moment.

"A few minutes of hailstorm can chop off all the corn stalks and leave nothing in the field. They even kill cattle, too."

"Do you have many such hailstorms around here?" he asked, curiously.

"Well, we certainly get more than our share. My car is liberally dented from hailstones."

Another customer called and Lisa had to go. Kenji finally had a moment to relax and take a deep and thoughtful breath for the first time since the early afternoon's calamity. In his mind now was nothing to do with the Porsche's mechanical problems, or his father's predictably nationalistic attitude, or even the depth of his longing for the forbidden Swedish girl, Inga. He was thinking of the mysterious openness of the locale in which he found himself. He was thinking of the exaggerated wide-open nothingness called Nebraska. Nothing in Japan had prepared him to witness such a thing with his own eyes and feel it with his own senses. It isn't really nothingness since corn grows everywhere, he thought. It resembled the basic human concept of nothingness because it had no rolling hills, no forests, no fences, no limits of any kind. This place (and he hadn't even really seen it yet) is, truly, an agricultural ocean — with all the expanse and freedom that term implies.

Kenji closed his eyes and let his mind fold in upon the wonders that assailed it.

Three

At 3:30 P.M. that afternoon, a handsome young man, wearing a cowboy hat with the sides of the brim rolled up tight, dusty white T-shirt and well-worn blue jeans, came into the restaurant. He had a tanned face, blue eyes and long blond hair.

"Hi, Lisa."

"Hi, George."

He kissed Lisa's cheek.

"This is Kenji."

"Nice to meet you," George put out his hand.

"Lisa said you might need a farm worker."

"Sure. We can always use one." George sat beside Kenji.

"Great."

"But my old man is a real slave-driver. You don't mind hard work?"

"No."

"How long you gonna stay?"

"I can't tell now. It all depends on how soon I can make enough money to repair the Porsche."

"I see."

"Everything is uncertain."

"Don't worry. Things will get better. Did you have lunch?"

"Yeah, I've eaten."

"Hey Lisa," George called out, "I'll have an order of

fries!" Turning to Kenji, he asked. "Why don't you have something?"

"An ice cream...vanilla."

"An ice cream...vanilla!" George called out.

While they waited, Kenji said to George, "Lisa said you don't like farming."

"No. As soon as I find something better, I'm gone."

"What do you want to be?"

"Anything except a farmer."

The orders arrived.

"Los Angeles is a very big place, isn't it?" asked George while downing his french fries.

"Very big."

"Must be very exciting."

"Lots of action, yes."

"I wish I could go there someday."

"Maybe you will."

After they finished, Kenji tried to pay but George said no.

They left the restaurant and entered George's electric-blue 1969 Chevy.

On the country highway, George drove fast passing the flat cornfields on both sides of the road, as heavy-metal rock music blared from the radio.

"What do you think of Lisa?" he asked.

"She's beautiful."

"She has been entered in the summer beauty contest this month at G.I."

"What's G.I.?"

"Grand Island."

"Oh."

"Kenji, do you have a girlfriend?"

"Yeah."

"In Japan?"

"No. In L.A."

"Is she American?"

"Yes."

"What's her name?"

"Inga. Inga Svenson."

"Nice name. Do you love her?"

"Very much. But my father wants me to marry a Japanese girl when I return home."

"What does Inga think about that?"

"She loves me and she wants to marry me when we're both finished with school."

"What is she studying?"

"Computer engineering, same as me, at U.S.C."

"Good."

"But I may have to drop school temporarily if I can't pay the tuition any more."

"Doesn't your family send you the money?"

"Yes, they did. But, if I don't stop dating Inga, they won't. My father hates mixed marriage."

"My father hates my girlfriend, Lisa, because she's a towny. He wants me to marry a farm girl. We're alike, Kenji."

"Our fathers are wrong."

"How about Inga's parents? Do they like you?"

Kenji began to think, his expression changed. "In the beginning they didn't like their daughter going out with an Oriental man but now they are beginning to understand."

"Good. Do you intend to go back to Japan whether you finish school or not?"

"I have two choices — either to drop Inga and go back to Japan after school or abandon my family and start a new life with her here in America."

"That's a tough choice."

"I know. Anyway, I have to make a decision."

Now George turned to the right and drove along the farm road, dirt blowing behind the car as the loud rock music continuously boomed from the radio. And now Kenji became excited. He could see a herd of grazing black-and-white cows corralled in a green pasture behind barbed-wire.

"How many cows do you have?"

"One hundred twenty with forty two calves."

Turning left at a tall silver mailbox — covered with American sticker flags — they drove up a twisting dirt driveway that led to a large, two-story farmhouse. The house was painted white, with a red chimney on a green-shingled roof. It was surrounded by several farm buildings and many trees. Behind was a tall silo which stood like a missile against the blue sky. On the right was a corn field that seemed to spread to infinity.

As Kenji exited the car, he heard the powerful sound of a motor approaching them. It was a green, muddy John Deere tractor that appeared stark and intruding with its steel blue smoke streaming out of the rusty exhaust pipe standing on the engine. The driver was a large man. He wore a bright red baseball cap slanted to the right, a dusty white T-shirt, blue jeans and muddy boots. Sitting on the right fender was a young boy dressed about the same, except his cap was green.

Henry, George's father, peered down intensely from the top of the tractor at Kenji as he brought the tractor to a halt near the car, stopping the roar of the engine.

"Are you the guy having trouble with his car?" Henry asked in a deep voice.

"Yes."

"How long can you work?"

"For two or three weeks. Or maybe more."

"You're too skinny. I don't think you can handle farm work."

"I need the job."

"Come on, Dad," said George, "you know we could use another hand. Any hand. It's a help."

"George, another peep out of you." Henry scowled at his son, "And I'll find enough chores to keep you away from your town girl permanently."

"Dad," said the younger boy who was still sitting on the tractor, "I don't like to cross you, but George is right. We've been needing a hired hand ever since Mike left. At least you could check him out." Henry seemed to listen more to the younger boy than to George.

"If I give you the job, I have the right to fire you without pay whenever I feel you aren't doing the job. All right?"

"Fine," said Kenji. He smiled.

Henry looked at the younger boy. "Remember that, son."

"Yeah," added George, "take notes, Johnny boy. Otherwise, you'll end up a dumb farmer like..."

"Shut up, George," said the younger boy. "You got a big mouth sometimes."

"Now, how much pay were you thinking of?"

"I was thinking of about $150 a week," replied Kenji, with a straight face.

Henry's eyes widened and he stopped breathing. Finally, he replied. "Has this sun made you crazy, boy?"

"No."

"How about $50 a week with room and board?"

"That's not even minimum wage."

"I don't even get minimum wage as the owner of this place."

Kenji hesitated a moment, then replied. "$100 a week with one day off."

Henry laughed at him with derision. "This is a dairy farm, boy. You want the cows to take a day off, too?"

Kenji felt confident. "If the cows are stupid enough to work every day of the year, I feel sorry for them. But you're really working for the cows, aren't you?"

Henry seemed didn't know whether to be upset or amused. "Me work for the cows?" His face turned red, but then it broke into a smile and he began to laugh, a long, hearty laugh. "You have a point there. I'm the employee and the cows are the boss. But I'm a farmer, so don't forget that. How about $70 a week, with no days off?"

"All right," agreed Kenji.

Henry climbed down from the tractor, with the younger boy, and put out his hand. "My name is Henry Harris. You can call me Henry. What's yours?"

"Kenji. Kenji Shimada." Kenji shook Henry's large calloused hand. He smiled. He felt a bit better about his financial problems. Yet, somehow he still felt angry with himself for arguing with his father on the phone and frustrated about not being able to move on his schedule to deliver the car.

"This is my son, John."

Kenji put out his hand to John. They shook hands.

Introductions over, Henry said, "Kenji, I want you to do one thing for me." Together they stood under a cool shaded cottonwood tree. "My son George is a pretty wild kid. I just want you to agree that you won't talk to George about California, no matter what. I don't want him running off somewhere."

"All right, I won't," he agreed.

"He'll eventually come around to my way of thinking, but it's gonna take awhile. You understand?"

"I understand."

The two boys were sitting on the front porch of the house when Henry and Kenji approached them.

"Is it a deal?" asked John excitedly.

"Yep," said Henry.

At that moment, a slim woman appeared behind the screen door of the porch.

John turned around and motioned. "Hey Mom, come on out and meet our new hired hand."

The woman, whose deep reddish-brown hair was almost the same color as her deeply tanned cheeks, came out onto the porch. "Hi," she said as she wiped her hands on her apron before shaking hands with Kenji. "My name is Mary. I'm Henry's wife. What's your name?"

"Kenji Shimada."

"What a beautiful name. Does it mean anything?"

"Kenji — ken means health and ji means two. Something like that. It doesn't have any special meaning...It's just my first name. As for my last name...shima means island and da means farm field."

"Is that why you're on a farm near Grand Island?"

"I never thought of that. That's pretty good."

"Kenji, I'll fatten you up while you're here. You're too skinny."

"O.K." Kenji smiled.

"Why don't you get Kenji situated and then have him come over to the milking barn?" called Henry as he and the boys left for the barn.

Mary escorted Kenji into the house. As he stepped on the hard plastic mat that covered the entrance to the living room, he became surprised at how sparkling clean and new everything looked. As he stepped off of the plastic mat and onto the fluffy white carpet, his foot felt as if it were sinking into a soft pillow. The furniture was all overstuffed and also very soft-looking. To the far left, he caught a glimpse of the kitchen. And at the right wall he saw a stone fireplace. A model of an old sailing ship sat in the center of the mantel with photographs on both sides. A dozen photographs were displayed on the shelf along above the mantel and the end tables displayed dozens of photographs that flanked the fireplace. Kenji recognized a picture of George in a cap and gown and another young man, who looked like Henry, also in a cap and gown. On the table was a picture of George in a purple tuxedo posing with Lisa, also in purple, including a large corsage of purple flowers on her wrist. On the other table, was a picture of the young man, who looked like Henry, standing with a very long-haired small Asian woman who was holding a baby. Kenji was amazed at how many pictures were crowded around the fire-place. To him, it looked like some type of religious decoration, except that he recognized some of the people as being still alive.

Mary was taking Kenji upstairs.

"Which part of Japan you from, Kenji?"

"Tokyo."

"It's a big city, right?"

"Yes, it's a big, crowded city. If you like it here in the country, you would hate Tokyo."

"That might be."

She opened one of the doors of the rooms.The once dark hallway filled with bright sunlight coming from the doorway of the room.

They stepped into a bedroom. The walls were a light pastel blue with a dark wooden trim on the baseboards and door. Up to the right, as he entered, was a set of deer antlers and beneath were three single-loading hunting rifles on a gun-rack on the wall.

"This is where you'll stay."

"It's a nice room," said Kenji. He put down his bag on the brightly polished wooden floor.

"This is my oldest son, Mike's room. And you are the first one to stay in his room since he left." She held up a big color gold-framed portrait which stood on the night table. "He's in the Navy now." She handed it to Kenji. "This is Mike."

Looking at the photograph of smiling Mike in his white Navy uniform, Kenji recognized him as Henry's son. He was a striking resemblance to Henry. "How old is he?"

"Twenty-two."

"He is two years older than me."

"I see."

"I think his eyes are exactly like yours," Kenji said. His eyes were a silver-gray color similar to Mary's. "But his bone structure is exactly like Henry's."

"Really?" she put the picture back as Kenji handed it back. "Nobody else has said that about Mike. You're very observant. You remind me of him."

Kenji could see that she was sad and her eyes revealed

her love. Kenji wanted to say something simple but he just couldn't.

"I miss Mike a lot. But I'm glad you're here."

"Maybe I'll see him someday."

"He'll be back soon."

"This summer?"

"No. He will be home this fall. He never misses the hunting season."

"I've never been hunting. I wouldn't like killing animals."

"Neither would I," said Mike's mother.

"Are those his?" Kenji asked, pointing to the hunting rifles on the wall.

"Yes," she said. "His father gave him one of them when he was twelve years old."

"Why was he given a gun at so young age?"

"All farm-boys have guns."

"In Japan, people don't own rifles. Only hunters with licenses have guns in Japan. In Los Angeles kids have guns, but they often use them to kill other kids. Aren't you afraid to give guns to children?"

"No. Farm children are more responsible."

"Yes, I suppose you're right."

"In Japan, do both of your parents work?"

"Just my father. My mother is a housewife."

"What kind of work does your father do?"

"He is an architect."

"Sounds like he is a rich man since he pays your tuition at U.S.C. and all your expenses."

"Not really."

"In the United States, many students get scholarships, or work during the summer."

"My girlfriend works in a restaurant as a waitress and types term papers for extra money. She studies computer engineering like me."

"Is she Japanese, too?"

"No, she is an American."

"A white girl?"

"Yes. She has blue eyes and blonde hair. It is white color like rice."

"How old is she?"

"Nineteen."

"Same as George. What does her family think of you?"

"They're supportive."

"If you marry her, will you take her to Japan?"

"No...because my father disapproves."

"Does she speak Japanese?"

"No. She speaks English and Swedish."

"Do most people know English in Japan."

"Today many young people can speak English. But most of them can't."

"So maybe you will live in America."

"Maybe," he agreed.

"What's your last name again?"

"Shimada."

"So if she marries you, her name would be...?"

"Inga Shimada."

"It sounds funny to me."

"I thought Americans like mixed marriages."

"Most Americans don't like it. But in time they learn to accept it if their children have a mixed marriage."

"In Los Angeles, everybody seems to mix races. But my father thinks mixed-marriage is disgusting."

"Well, the people from California are considered weird around here."

"Maybe you're right. In Nebraska, it looks like everyone is the same race...white. In Los Angeles, the people came from all over the world."

"I hope you don't think I'm a racist, Kenji. But, I'm from Nebraska. I've lived here all my life. When you live around here you get to think a certain way. You understand what I'm saying?"

"Yes. My father is the same way. He has lived in Japan all his life and has never been out of the country. But my uncle Kazuyoshi thinks differently because he travels overseas a lot, mainly in Asia. Does Mike travel much in the Navy?"

"Yeah, he does."

"Does he like the Navy?"

"He loves the Navy. He likes ships. He's crazy about them," she said and smiled. "He made a lot of ship models. He also made that ship." She pointed to a ship on the desk. "I think he called it a three-masted bark. He made it all by hand."

Kenji was impressed. He counted eighteen cloth sails on three of the masts and there were a lot of triangular sails at the front and back. He imagined that it must have taken long hours of patience to carve out all of the wooden details, sew the sails, and thread all of the riggings.

"He must be a very handy man."

"He spent many a winter day building model ships when the farm was slow."

Kenji smiled. "Do you know where he is now?"

"Somewhere out in the Pacific Ocean. He's on the aircraft carrier Kittyhawk. It's like a small island."

"Not like a Grand Island?" Kenji said jokingly.

"No. Because there aren't any farms on that aircraft carrier," she returned.

"Does he like the farm very much?"

"He hates it. But my husband would kill him if he left for good."

"Why?"

"Because Henry wants his sons to be farmers. And what Henry wants Henry gets. He is a very stubborn man, stubborn like a bull," she laughed. "And my second son, George, is also as stubborn as his father. But I don't think George will be here very much longer. Henry wants George to be a farm woman's husband."

"Was Mike the same way?"

"No. Eventually he'll be back and he'll stay forever."

"So Mike and John will work on the farm in the future?"

"That's what I'm thinking. How many brothers and sisters do you have?"

"Only one older brother. He works for an electronics company."

"Does he travels a lot, too?"

"No, he doesn't have time for himself, only for his company."

"That's too bad. Kenji, if you have clothes to wash leave them on the floor. I'll wash them tomorrow morning."

"All right," he said. "May I use your telephone to make a collect call to Japan?"

"Sure. Go ahead."

"I will call a little later." Kenji knew it was about six o'clock in the morning in Japan.

"O.K."

After Mary left, Kenji sat at the desk as he took out his pocketbook from his pocket. He opened it to look at the contract again, but he took out the picture of smiling Inga, instead. He stared into her light blue eyes. He missed her badly. He missed playing with her soft bobbed platinum-blond. He remembered how her soft full lips felt. He looked at her face with tenderness. He felt happy knowing that she was so different from anyone he had ever known. But now the two extreme choices facing him came to mind again and he wanted to cry as he put the picture down on the desk. And then his face was in his hands.

He hurried downstairs, into the living room, and made a collect call to Japan.

His mother, Kumiko, answered the phone.

"Mom, this is Kenji."

"Kenji, your father wants you to marry a Japanese girl when you return to Japan after finishing your education in America."

"Mom, I love Inga. But I don't want to talk about that now. The reason I called is to let you know I'm all right. I'm staying with an American farm family."

"How long have you known them?"

"I just met them a few hours ago."

"Are you sure it's safe to stay there with them?"

"They are very friendly and helpful."

"*Shinyo shicha ikenai* (you shouldn't trust anybody). Why don't you stay in a hotel?"

"I am working for seventy dollars a week, including room and board. So I can save enough money to get the car fixed."

"I hear all the time about Japanese getting killed for their money in foreign countries."

"Don't worry about me. I've been living in America for three years and I understand Americans. They are very, very friendly.

"I hear on television, Americans have guns. So they are shooting people all the time."

Kenji thought about the rifles in Mike's room. For a moment he felt a little bit nervous, but he knew that his mother had a *shinpai-sho* (worry habit).

"I promise you, Mom, at the first sign of trouble I'll leave."

"Your father will be home after ten o'clock tonight. I want you to call as soon as you can. I will try to convince him to send you the money." Kenji's mother began crying, barely able to speak, "Otherwise I won't get any sleep."

Kenji felt tears running down his cheeks. He wasn't sure if it was because his mother wasn't happy with him, or because for the moment he felt homesick. With a choked voice he said, "I will call. And I will be careful," he hung up the phone.

Thinking about his breaking out of the tradition of his family he felt very pained. He tried to put it all out of his mind as he left by the front door of the living room. He checked the knob after closing the door to be sure it was locked. It was then he noticed the doorknob didn't even have a lock on it.

Four

At four, the cows had already gathered around the large white barn for their second milking of the day. Kenji entered into a lean-to that was built on to the structure and used for a milking room. It also faced the kitchen door of the house, across the farmyard. The milking room was clean and bright with sunlight that flowed in through a large window that offered a view of the corral. A spotless, stainless steel milk tank was positioned in the middle, and Kenji's reflection on the polished steel made him appear as if he were standing in front of a fun-house mirror.

"Hi, John," Kenji said, as he saw the young boy walk out from behind the milk tank.

"Kenji, do you have cows in Japan?"

"Of course, we do. On the northern island of Hokkaido, there are many dairy farms like this."

"I see."

"John, do you really want to be a farmer?"

"Yep. I like farming. I love riding tractors."

"It's not easy being a farmer these days, is it, John?"

"I know," said John, walking over to where a number of octopus-like machines were stored. "But it's still worth the effort. Kenji, these are milking machines and we have to take them into the milk barn." He picked up two of them. "Just grab a couple and follow me."

"All right," Kenji said. He picked up the strange equipment he had never seen before and followed John into the milk barn, where the smell of hay and manure assaulted Kenji's nose. He closed his eyes for a moment to adjust to the lack of light, and to the many flies buzzing about him.

After they set the milking machines in the stalls, John turned on the lights.

"Kenji, your job will be to lead the cows through the door..." he pointed far off to the opened wooden half-door at the corner, "...into here." He pointed down to the dirt floor covered with dry straws. "When one cow is finished being milked and leaves the stall," he gestured, "you let one of the other cows in."

"All right."

"It's very simple and the cows will help you with your job."

Kenji reluctantly walked into the back barn through the heavy half-door with John leading the way. Kenji hated the acrid smell of manure mixed with dirty hay.

"John," Kenji called out.

John looked back.

"Look at my boots." Kenji pointed down to his nice lizard-skin boots sucked deep into the piles of manure.

"Don't worry about it. When it dries, you can just brush it off. But be careful that you don't slip in it."

Kenji walked carefully to avoid slipping as John pushed the large sliding door, which emitted an ominous rumbling sound.

A clear, blue sky appeared above the cows who were jammed together and standing anxiously. The mouths of their gentle faces still ground cud with a slow rhythm; foam formed around those mouths as if they were glasses of warm beer. One cow even rested her head on another cow's bony back. Behind this crowd of cows, others stood silently and patiently, waiting to be milked, swaying their tails energetically against their sides to chase away flies. At the edge of the corral stood a tall, regal cottonwood which cast a long shadow that had several cows in it. Those cows seemed utterly passive and patient.

Then Kenji noticed the cows hesitating to enter. They saw the stranger — Kenji. They would try to back up but couldn't, since so many others were jammed behind.

"Hey, come on in!" shouted John at the cows, the loud rock music that was playing drowning him out.

But the animals still hesitated to enter.

"Kenji, you better hide behind me," said John while he held open the door. "They're nervous, if they see strange people."

Kenji stood quietly behind him.

"Hey, you guys come on in!"

Finally, the cows came into the back barn very slowly and cautiously; each made a sharp turn at the opened half-door, and disappeared into the milk barn. It was apparent the animals knew their routine.

"Now, I'll go and close the door and you fill this back barn with the next group of cows," John said as he walked to the half-door, after the eighth cow came through and disappeared into the milk barn.

"All right."

John closed the half-door.

In the back barn, the ninth cow seemed to know to wait its turn.

Kenji tried to put some more cows into the back barn as he hid himself behind the sliding door. But the cows still hesitated to enter. "Come in," Kenji urged them, "come in."

Finally, Kenji thought to himself.

When the back barn was filled with cows, Kenji closed the heavy sliding door. He gently touched ribs of one of the big black-and-white cows as he carefully walked among them toward the closed half-door. He felt warm as he touched her.

Returning to the milk barn, he watched John hook up

milk cups to the teats of a cow. George had joined John and was helping. The milking machine hung down from a curved iron bar, underneath the cow's belly, which belted to the thick leather strap encircling her body.

John quickly moved over to help George attach the remaining milk cups to the other cows.

George, John and the cows all seemed to know their jobs perfectly. The silence among all of them seemed to be a sign of mutual respect and cooperation.

The cows seemed very nonchalant about the whole process. In the stalls, they looked peaceful, their heads buried in a long wooden feeding-trough and their tails lazily moving back and forth; the cows were giving and the milkers were taking.

Kenji noticed that all the cows were chained around their rear legs.

"Why did you chain them all?" Kenji asked John.

"Because a cow's hoof packs a mean wallop."

"What's a wallop?"

John laughed. He hit a fist against his other hand. "Pow!"

"This is why," said George, lifting up his shirt.

Kenji moved closer to him and saw a horseshoe-shaped scar on his right side.

"Does it still hurt?"

"Naw, no big deal."

Now John deftly loosened the chain from the rear legs of a cow he had been milking, after which he removed the milking machine, and fastened it to another cow. Then he took off the leather strap around her body and then pulled a long metal pin to release her.

"One more cow, Kenji," said John.

As she trotted out into the corral, Kenji slid the half-door open to let in one more cow, but a second attempted to enter, too. He tried to stop her forward progress, but was having no success at all. The door even leaned to one side as the cow tried to force her way into the milk barn. He pushed hard to hold the gate straight with both his hands but she wouldn't move back even one inch. It looked like a stand-off until George interceded and casually struck the cow in her gleaming, black, watery eyes with his fingers. The cow then scurried backward into the back barn.

"Doesn't that hurt her eyes?" asked Kenji. He was concerned for the cow.

"It's the only way to get them to back up. Next time a cow won't move for you, you hit 'em just like I did," said George.

"There're better ways to handle a cow, Kenji," advised John.

"No way!" shouted the older brother.

"Boys, boys," came another voice. Mary, who wore blue jeans, long waterproof rubber shoes and with her hair in a scarf, entered.

"Kenji," she counseled, "if a cow tries to get in, just brush your hand fast in front of her eyes." She moved her hand in front of her face in a brushing motion to demonstrate. "That will move her back."

George's method certainly worked, but Kenji liked the fact that there was another way to intimidate a cow.

With fascination Kenji watched the milk squirt into the clear milking jars below the cows' teats. To Kenji it was a wondrous new sight and sound. "You know," he said, "this reminds me of the oil wells in California...sucking the oil out of the ground and pumping it through the pipes into the tanks."

"Milk is the dairy farmer's oil," said John, with a smile. "It's white oil!"

"I wish we were pumping oil instead of milk," said George. "Then we'd all be sitting by a swimming pool in a luxury hotel, sipping cocktails, instead of standing here up to our ankles in cow shit!"

"Manure makes rich soil!" boomed a deep voice from

the other side of the barn.

Henry came into the barn. But, instead of going to the stalls to milk, he made a right turn toward a dark corner, fiddling with the barn radio knobs. Then, suddenly, the barn was filled with country music.

"I hate country," muttered George, loud enough for everyone, especially Henry, to hear.

"You know, Kenji, this is my type of music! Country! K.R.V.N. Lexington, Nebraska! They play country all day. It's the rich kind of country!"

"I used to listen to it in L.A."

"Los Angeles country is city country! It's not the same as country country music."

Mary laughed. "If Kenji knows the same songs, then what difference does it make where he hears them?"

"Ssshh!" commanded Henry, as another song came on the radio. It was some obscure song about farmers, tractors and mortgages.

"I've never heard that one before," said Kenji.

"See?" said Henry proudly. "This is real country music, about real problems and real people. Not some tight ass Hollywood type country song," said Henry as he worked at the far end of the barn. John stood working at the opposite end of the barn by the half-door and George worked in the center while Mary flitted about.

"You know, Kenji, cows love country, too. It helps them relax and then they produce a lot more milk."

"That's an old wives' tale," said John. "Scientifically speaking, they..."

"That's enough from you, boy."

"Yes, Dad," John said. He unchained his cow.

Kenji allowed a cow to walk into an empty stall and let more cows into the back barn. He then shut the door and returned to the milk barn.

"Kenji, what's your favorite kind of music?" asked Mary.

"I like jazz. When I get to New York I hope I can enjoy some good jazz."

"Give me a break," groaned Henry. "If it's not country, it's not music!"

Kenji sent in one more cow which had a written number 5 on her side.

"Here's mother No.5," said Mary, passing a plastic bucket with that number to John.

"What's the numbered bucket for?"

"This cow just had a calf," explained John, milking her with his hands and filling the bucket. "The calf is kept over in the pen. When we're finished, we'll go over and feed the calf its mother's own milk from the bucket. Are you getting the idea, Kenji?"

"Can't you use any milk?"

"Yeah, you could. But then the calf wouldn't be so well-adjusted when it grows up. It wouldn't grow as big as it could be, either. After three weeks," John nearly filled the bucket with her milk, "they can have any kind of milk. But the first three weeks is very important for the calf."

"I see."

A cow turned around very quickly just after entering into the milk barn and faced toward Kenji. Kenji felt threatened as if a bull was challenging him in a bullring. He quickly stepped into an empty stall until the cow walked out into the back barn.

"Are you all right, Kenji?" asked Mary worriedly.

"I'm all right," said Kenji. "But she scared me."

"You go and drive her back in here," Henry said to Kenji as he handed him a meter-long stick. "Take this one. You'll need it."

In the back barn, the cow moved nervously. Mooing, she panicked when Kenji struck her to drive her out of the back barn to be milked.

Henry quickly approached the back barn. "Kenji, not so rough! You don't have to use force! Just show her the stick to guide her. That's all."

Kenji used the stick in the way Henry told him and it worked. The cow left and entered the milk barn.

"Remember," said Henry. "If the cows panic or get excited, they produce less milk.'

"The most important thing for the cows is to feed them well, keep them calm and comfortable, and treat them very gently...like a woman," advised Henry. Kenji smiled.

"I think there's a lot I have to learn," said Kenji, trying to sound as humble as he felt.

"If you watch cows carefully at milking, there are a lot of things you can learn. First of all, you can see that they follow set patterns. You know, this is Daisy," said Henry, patting the rump of a cow, which just now went into the milking stall, "She is always the seventy-fourth to be milked. She never makes a mistake!"

"Do you mean that each cow knows her place in the milking line?"

"You bet," Henry said. "They do. The last cow is always Jill."

"That's amazing. How do they know how to keep the same order?"

"I don't know, exactly," answered Henry. "I guess they know each other by smell."

"I'll watch them carefully tomorrow."

"You should. They have their own leader, too. Her name is Boss. And they're very cooperative. They even take care of each other. Would you believe one will even baby sit another's calf if she goes for water?"

"Hard to believe that," Kenji sent in another cow.

"But some are not so cooperative," said Mary, pushing the cow's hip to move it into the stall. "Like this one."

Kenji quickly helped Mary. Together they were pushing the cow.

"This is a big one. It's like pushing a boulder on a mountain," said Kenji as he threw his weight against the animal.

"You see," said Mary calmly, after the cow was secured in the stall. "Cows can be really stubborn," Mary added as she wiped the cow's dirty teats with a wet towel. At this time, the cow hit Mary's face with her long wet tail. "Oh, no!" she cried. Taking a handkerchief out of her back pocket she wiped her wet face as George attached the milking machine. "You know," she added, "in winter when they do that it's worse. Because their tails contain ice chunks that can really hurt you."

"I can imagine," said Kenji.

"It sure wakes you up during the early morning milk," said Henry. Except George, everybody laughed.

Kenji opened and closed the heavy half-door many times. Mary retired from milking to prepare dinner.

Another mother cow came in. George filled the numbered plastic bucket with her milk, like John had done earlier.

Then, while George was attaching the milk cups to the cow, Kenji carried the bucket out to the milk room but dropped it and spilled half of the milk.

"Damn!" shouted Henry. "You're not concentrating on your work!"

"I'm very sorry," said Kenji. "It won't happen again."

"Thank God..." whispered George, as he was refilling the bucket, "...I didn't spill it."

The evening milking was nearly over. Through the door, Kenji saw birds wheeling in the rosy sky of a sunset above the flat horizon.

A while later, the last cow entered. She lumbered in with her huge heavy udders swaying.

"This is Jill. I always milk her," said Henry, with some pride, to Kenji. "You know why?"

"No."

"Because I can tell her my problems. She listens well without talking back."

"I see," Kenji smiled.

Seemingly Henry poured his heart out to her, as she just

stood there, with that somber, placid face, taking it all in. She nodded every once in a while like any good bartender or psychiatrist. Henry and Jill almost seemed to be commiserating with each other. They even look a bit alike, Kenji thought.

After milking Jill, Henry left the barn.

"Damn boring music!" George groaned as he changed the radio station. Rock 'N' Roll now blared loudly. If the cows had still been there, thought Kenji, they would have been frightened beyond words.

One hundred and twenty cows had paraded in during the two and half hours. Kenji was tired, both physically and emotionally.

George cleaned out the manure in the milk barn with a pitchfork and then dropped a bale of hay from upstairs through an opening in the roof made for a ladder.

In the calf pen, next to the milk barn, were many young calves, mooing softly, with numbers on their sides corresponding to their mothers and the numbers on the buckets. As John and Kenji got into the pen many calves began to gather around them; they each carried two buckets in their hands.

To Kenji the calves looked very sad being separated from their mothers. "Why don't you just isolate the calf and mother together?"

"That's no good because they'd suck all the time and make themselves sick."

Kenji nodded as John tapped the calves' heads with a rod to drive them all away except for the four they wanted. Kenji heard the hollow tapping sound of the rod against the calves' skulls. He was surprised at how loud it was.

"Kenji," John called, "hold this bucket."

As Kenji held up the bucket, John pushed a calf's head deep down forcefully into the milk bucket, putting two fingers into the calf's mouth to urge drinking. "Come on!" urged John. "Drink! Drink!" The calf began to suck.

Kenji saw the milk level going down quickly. "John," he said, "doesn't she know how to drink by herself?"

"No. She only knows how to suck, but not to drink. So, we have to teach her how to drink. She thinks my fingers are teats so she sucks now. But in a couple of days she will learn how to drink from the bucket without the fingers."

Quickly the calf sucked the bucket dry.

"Wow, she really drank a lot," said Kenji. "She must be hungry."

"They're always hungry."

"Can I try?" Kenji was very eager.

"Sure. Get number five and try."

Kenji picked up the number five bucket, and as John held up the bucket, Kenji fed calf number five, who was the smallest of all. Letting it suck his finger he felt good. When it was finished, he rubbed its broad, furry head.

While John and Kenji were feeding calves, George put away the milking equipment into the milk room.

Finally they turned off the radio, the lights, and closed the doors to darkness. The barn returned to silence again.

The three of them stomped their boots to clean off the manure as they walked toward the house.

As they neared the house, Kenji smelled good food. He was very hungry.

After they entered from the side door, they all took off their soiled boots and placed them in a line on the floor against the wall. Newspapers were put underneath the boots. Thinking of the Japanese custom where people take off their shoes in *genkan* (vestibules) before entering the rooms, Kenji felt, in a peculiar, if not distant way, that Nebraska and Japan were not all that different.

Now, before having dinner, they all delightfully rushed into the two bathrooms, one after another, to take showers.

During the time he awaited his turn for the bathroom, Kenji had his first chance that day to just close his eyes and think. This was such a far cry from anything he had ever seen — much less attempted to do, it was as if he had temporarily stepped onto a different planet. He knew that Japanese farmers (in up-country Hokkaido) also owed and made a living from dairy cows, but, probably, he thought, it wasn't nearly the same thing as this. For reasons he could not verbalize — or even understand — clearly, Kenji was certain the Japanese farmers were simply not as close to their cows as were these Nebraskans. In a word, those Japanese dairy farmers somehow maintained a distance from their animals — an aloofness, even. They may have walked ankle-deep in smelly manure just the same as these Nebraskans did, but they nevertheless held to some of the same separateness as the samurai of old.

Yes, he thought, there is a striking sameness as well as a startling difference in the two farming cultures. And yet, the end product is the same. They each produce milk, children, debts as an occasional laugh...as well as an occasional tear.

Five

The smell of sweet corn filled the house. The table was set with a sparkling white tablecloth that was severely contrasted by the dirty clothes worn by the men. The table itself showcased mountains of fried chicken, vegetables, and hot biscuits with gravy. Kenji noticed that Henry's face was deeply tanned, except for his forehead where the shade of his cap had been. His hair was gray and short.

"Do you like corn, Kenji?" asked Mary.

"Yes, very much."

"It's too sweet for me," she replied.

"Kenji, everything at this table is real honest-to-God American food!" Henry said very proudly.

"Someone told me once that ketchup came from China," Kenji responded, pointing to the ketchup.

"But tomatoes came from America." Kenji then passed a large hot bowl of potatoes to Henry, who went on, "Same as these potatoes. And this corn. And those beans over there. Most of the food eaten in the world today originally came from the Indians in America."

"I didn't know that."

"Did you know that when the first Europeans stepped foot on Plymouth Rock the Indians had a bowl of popcorn waiting for them?"

George let out a suppressed laugh.

Henry went on, "America has given more to this world than any other civilization. Did you know that Thomas Jefferson, an American, developed the first efficient mold-board?"

"What's that?" Kenji asked.

"It's the curved portion of the plow that turns over the soil. The coulter and plowshare cuts into the earth, but after making the furrow, the loosened earth needs to be turned over. It was Jefferson who made this development. Also, there was another man, name of McCormick, who developed an efficient reaper. The Japanese companies, Japahatchy, Hitacho, Sonya, or whatever, can make a cheaper product. But they can't compete with good old American know-how. That's why I only use John Deere machinery on my farm."

"I heard that American tools are the best," Kenji said.

"Damn right!"

After Henry said that, John chuckled.

"What's so funny?" asked Henry.

John answered, "Oh, just something funny I heard today. What you were saying reminded me of it."

"Oh. Well, share it with us."

Still smiling, John replied, "Did you hear about the tractor salesman whose wife left him?"

"I'll bite," said Henry. "What about him?"

"The guy came home from work and found a John Deere letter waiting for him."

There was only a smattering of laughter, after which everyone returned to the job at hand — eating.

As the meal progressed even George and Henry started to get along more like father and son.

"Don't you like chicken?" Mary asked Kenji. "You haven't eaten much of it."

"I had enough. I like vegetables."

"Vegetarians be damned!" said Henry.

"Cows are vegetarians," said John quietly.

"They'd better be," replied Henry without missing a beat, or a bite, "because they're too clumsy to chase down their food."

John watched Kenji to determine if he handled his table ware differently.

"How do you eat with chopsticks?" he asked.

Kenji held his dish high up in his hand close to his mouth, pantomiming with invisible chopsticks.

"Mom, do we have anything like chopsticks?" asked John. "I want Kenji to teach me how to use them."

Henry answered, "We have some quarter-inch dowel rods in the basement. You can practice after dinner."

John started wolfing down his dinner.

"There will be plenty of time after we've eaten," Henry yelled. "Slow down!"

John did. Then to Kenji, "Why did you come to America?"

"To learn about other cultures and new things."

"Aren't you homesick?"

"The first year I was in America, yes. But I made many new friends, so I'm all right."

"Do you have a girlfriend?" John asked.

"Yes."

"Is she pretty?"

"Yes."

Just as John was about to ask another question, Mary said, "That's enough, John. I'm sure Kenji doesn't want you asking so many questions."

John finished the last of his dinner. He then excused himself from the table and went down to the basement.

The enormous supply of food had quickly disappeared. Henry cleaned his dish with a piece of bread. Against his big brown hand, the dish looked very small.

As soon as George finished his meal, he rose from the

table.

"I promised Lisa I'd come over tonight," he said.

"You'll get home late again. And you won't be worth a damn tomorrow."

"Henry," interrupted Mary. "George is young. He'll be fine in the morning."

"Don't you dare stay out all night!" Henry called out, but George was already out the door.

John ran up the basement steps with the dowel rods.

"Can you show me how to eat with the chopsticks?" He asked Kenji.

"Sure." Kenji cut and shaped the dowel rods with his red Swiss Army pocket knife. He gave a pair of the new "chopsticks" to both Henry and John.

"First you put them in your right hand like this," Kenji demonstrated, holding the rest of a pair in his hand, "and then, holding them under your thumb, you hold this stick between the index and middle finger and the other against the ring finger."

John pulled some grapes from the fruit bowl on the table and placed them on a saucer. Henry and John chased the grapes around. John had hold of a grape and just as he brought it up to his mouth he squeezed the chopsticks too hard and the grape flew, hitting Henry's forehead. Henry laughed. Kenji was glad to see the rough exterior of Henry drop away to reveal the loving father beneath.

An hour passed before the two finally learned to use the chopsticks properly. Then the three of them retired to bed.

Six

Kenji entered his room. He turned on the light by the bed, then opened the window wide, allowing the soft night breeze to drift into the room. Looking out the window, he saw a vast corn field reflected in bright moonlight. The Nebraska night was serene and peaceful. Listening to the sound of the crickets in the distance he remembered an event that happened when he was seven. His father had given him four one-hundred yen coins. With the money he bought a cricket in a cage. He spent many happy nights listening to the sounds made by his new pet. The Nebraska crickets outside brought all those happy memories back. But the happy memories faded as the recent argument he had had with his father echoed in his memory.

In his dream that night Mike was sailing the ship he made. Kenji could see his parents waving to him from the side of the vessel. He wanted to thank Mike for bringing his parents to America so he could explain things to them. But, his mouth was not working. As they disembarked from the ship, he watched as the antlers above Mike's rifles began to take form — Henry was dressed like a viking with giant horns on his head, having six huge muscular arms like the Indian God Shiva. Kenji watched as Henry took the rifles off of the rack and each set of arms held them at Kenji.

47

Kenji's mother shouted out to the Shiva-armed Henry: *"Watashi no musuko o korosanai de kudasai* (Please don't kill my son)!" Inga came quickly to comfort her. His father stood with crossed arms looking at the women with his unhappy face. Again his mother screamed to Henry: *"Watashi no musuko o korosanai de kudasai!"* Kenji heard Henry cocking all three rifles, as he said, "Give me all your money or I will kill you." In the next instant, he saw the rifles explode into his face in a blinding flash. Through the high pitched screaming of the women and the explosions of the rifles, Kenji yelled at the top of his lungs,

"No...!"

At this time, there was an annoying ring from the alarm clock on the night table.

He shut off the alarm. He felt sweaty. He tried to sleep a few more minutes.

Then, there was a knocking at his door.

"Kenji, wake up!" It was Mary's voice. "It's time for the morning milking!"

What a life, Kenji said to himself. He hated to get up at such an early hour.

There was another a knocking sound.

"Kenji!"

"I will get up," said Kenji. He forced himself up.

He turned the light on. It was four-thirty. The ship was back on the desk. The antlers and the rifles were back on the wall.

When he got up he went to the window and looked out. It was dark and very quiet, as if the whole world were immersed in ink.

Seven

Kenji washed and dressed. He wore a clean red jacket over his T-shirt.

"Good morning, Mary."

"Good morning, Kenji."

As he sat at the table, Mary poured him a cup of steaming hot coffee. Kenji explained about his frightful dream.

"Kenji, I'll take those guns down later on and store them someplace else while you're staying here. That will make you more comfortable."

"Thank you," said Kenji, as he grabbed the warm coffee cup in his cold hands.

John was reading a magazine while munching on some muffins.

Now George came in and sat. He looked very sleepy.

"What time did you get in last night, George?" asked Mary, pouring coffee.

"Late," he mumbled.

"You really should take better care of yourself," said Mary.

He didn't say anything.

Then he said to Kenji in his sleepy voice, "Kenji, could you pass the sugar?" Kenji could not help but smell alcohol and cigarettes on George's breath.

"Here, George," said Kenji.

George put three heaping teaspoons of sugar in his coffee.

"That much sugar is bad for you," advised Kenji.

"Is that so?" answered George sarcastically, putting in another.

"He'll just do the opposite of whatever you tell him, Kenji," said John.

George told his younger brother to shut up. John went back to his magazine.

"Kenji, help yourself," said Mary.

Kenji picked up a warm flaky muffin and put some strawberry on it.

"It says here," announced John, "that soy beans are a better crop than corn for farms with our average rainfall. It could be a couple hundred dollars more per acre."

"Jesus," muttered George.

"Some farms in Iowa have converted to soy beans. And they're doing great!"

"Tell that to Dad," said George. "He'll love to hear that,"

"He might listen to me," said John, meekly.

"That's right, little brother. Our little do-no-wrong."

Kenji was eating a muffin. John was reading. George was dozing off.

"Wake up! Wake up! Wake up!" said Mary. "There's work to be done, boys. Let's hop to it!" Henry would have said it with more flair — and more profanity — but Mary got the message across.

"Damn!" George groaned. He pushed his chair back and stood. The other two also stood.

Everyone walked through the kitchen to the rack near the door where the colorful work clothes hung. George and John put their feet into their heavy and greasy cowboy boots, as did Kenji.

Now they heard Henry coming downstairs so Mary stayed behind and the boys went out hurriedly.

Outside, George, John and Kenji walked to the barn.

They could see their breath in the cold air. Kenji put his hands in his pockets and hunched his shoulders in order to keep warm.

George forced his body to open the barn door. Once inside, he turned on the lights and the radio, filling the barn with rock and roll music, as if to purposely assault the pre-dawn Nebraska morning. Everyone moved slowly trying to awaken themselves.

In the early morning, Kenji could not stand loud Rock 'N' Roll. Soothing jazz would have been his choice if any-one had asked. But no one had. So Kenji kept his mouth shut and helped set the machines in the milking stalls.

And so was readied the milk barn for the parade of one hundred and twenty cows.

A sliding door was rolled back.

"Good morning, ladies! Milking time!" shouted John to the herd of cows standing motionlessly in the darkness look-ing inside the bright barn.

To Kenji they looked anxious; to John they looked con-tented; to George they simply looked bored.

"I wish they could talk," said Kenji.

"I wish they could milk themselves!" groaned George.

George finished with his cow, loosened the chain, unstrapped the leather belt, and unhooked the pin. He worked on another cow as Kenji sent in another to fill the empty stall.

Kenji got into the back barn, where there were only two left, to open the sliding door to bring in another group. He ran carefully to the sliding door. Visions of twenty cows trampling him as they all rushed at him at the same time filled his thoughts. He opened the door. One cow rushed in. Then another. And another. Four...five...eight...nine... When enough cows had gone past, he shut the door.

"Send in another!" hollered George. He sounded a bit like his father.

Kenji cheerfully but quietly did as he was told. He was

inordinately proud and confident of himself in this new job.

"Where's Dad?" asked George. "Shouldn't he be helping?"

"Mind your own beeswax, George," said Mary, sharply. "He needs his rest. He has been working too hard." To Kenji, the tone of her voice revealed that she loved Henry very much.

The barn was really warming up, the hard Rock 'N' Roll was on the radio, and — the station suddenly changed — now the cheerful country was on the radio.

George didn't even have to look up. He knew what had happened. Henry had entered.

"From the way you look, you came home after midnight again, didn't you?" Henry demanded of George.

George didn't speak, just kept on quietly milking.

"Listen, boy, you have an obligation to this farm, and, as I see it, you're not living up to it. Why can't you be like these cows? They stay on the farm, get up early every morning, they do their job, they..."

"Dear, leave him alone," Mary's soft voice replied.

Henry quickly lost himself in his work with the cows. He really seemed to enjoy milking.

Kenji admired the animals' orderly movement.

As the morning milking progressed, it got lighter and lighter outside, as the sun began to rise. Kenji took off his jacket and hung it up on a rusty nail on the wall. The others also took off their heavy shirts and hung them on the nails. The morning chill was gone, as well as the chill among the Harris family. Kenji had a feeling that George did not hate his father. He hated the farm life. Unfortunately, his father and the farm were very difficult to separate.

Now a soft engine sound filled the air.

"That's an aerial sprayer," said John to Kenji, pointing out through the sliding door a single-engine airplane dipping over neighboring fields. "Spraying pesticides."

"Why is he doing it so early?"

"When it gets hot, the air molecules move a lot faster, blowing everything away. That's why you have to do it while the air is still," explained John.

"We probably need another spraying ourselves," said Henry unhappily. "Too many damn grasshoppers this year."

"They eat a lot of crops," John said to Kenji sadly.

Kenji was more interested in watching the plane. It flew just above the cornfield as it released its spray, then rose again in the sky.

Mary excused herself to go home. This was a welcome sign which meant that the milking was half way through.

A while later, the last cow, Jill, lumbered through the door, waving her ugly long tail. Henry milked her.

Eight

After the morning milking, George, John, and Kenji strolled into the spacious kitchen, filled with the smell of cooking bacon. After hanging their caps on the wall they took off their muddy boots.

Kenji then called the international operator. Within minutes, his mother was on the phone.

"Hi, Mom. Kenji."

"Are you calling from a hotel?"

"No, I am still on my employer's farm. They are typical Americans...very nice. What about Dad? Did you talk to him?"

"Yes I did. He said that he would send you no money unless you promise to marry a Japanese girl. He is very upset with you. Because you are still *kanojo to tsukiatte iru kara* (going out with Inga). You are still a young man. Your emotions are still growing. In time you will grow to understand what he is saying."

Kenji wished he had the courage to shout to his mother to blow out his frustration. But he didn't. He couldn't. The reason was simple. His mother was a Japanese woman, and what he thought of the Oriental fair sex was not very complimentary. In a word, having been exposed to women of the Occidental world, Kenji now found Oriental women incapable of holding down a meaningful conversation about anything. Their conditioning to the male-dominated Japanese culture had taught them to say nothing except *hai* (yes), and *sensei* (master) and a few well-travelled tritenesses. He knew that she wouldn't pointed out her own opinion (about once she had approved Kenji to go out with Inga) clearly to his father. Kenji knew that she couldn't express her feeling to his father in keeping thousands old tradition of *sakaraccha ikenai* (not going against another's will or opinion). So, how could he yell to his mother? It was easier to simply agree with her.

"I understand, Mom. I think Inga and I may be able to compromise somehow."

"How long will you be working?"

"I don't know yet. Maybe two weeks. Maybe a month. And then I should know what I will decide. Don't worry about me. I know what I'm doing. I get paid."

Suddenly, his father's drunken voice was heard. "*Bakayaro* (foolish)! I hate you! Remember, *gaijin tachi* (foreigners) will destroy our blood! *Bakayaro*!...you've been brain-washed!"

Kenji hung up, worrying about his father. He could tell the man was quite drunk.

He walked over to the table that was covered with eggs, pancakes, bacon, ham, biscuits, gravy and so on...over a dozen plates and bowls. It looked as if Mary was expecting an Army.

He sat down silently. After Henry's blessing, the family began passing the dishes and bowls around the table, serving themselves. Kenji's mouth watered.

"John, don't forget to give the calves some cold water today," said Henry. "It's gonna be really hot."

John nodded in agreement.

"The weatherman said it's going to be about ninety degrees with high humidity," informed Mary.

"That'll break my back," complained George.

"You have to be tougher!" shot Henry.

"I don't have to be tougher, I just have to cope."

"You shouldn't eat so much in hot weather," said Henry.

"In Los Angeles," said Kenji with a smile, "we'd say that's a great beach day — a great tanning day."

"In Nebraska, you don't need a beach for a tan," said Henry. "Just spend a few days in the field and you'll get as black as licorice."

Kenji laughed and this seemed to have a relaxing effect on everyone. First George, then Henry, and then the whole family began laughing.

"So tell me, Kenji," Henry asked, between big bites of food. "Are there any farms like this in Tokyo?"

"Not in Tokyo. Tokyo is like New York. All buildings...a concrete jungle. In the northern island, called Hokkaido, there are many dairy farms."

"The rest of the country is what...rice?" asked Henry.

"Most of the country has small rice fields. But in Hokkaido they grow a lot of corn and potatoes. Very famous in Japan."

"Do they eat corn and potatoes in Japan?" asked John.

"Of course. The Japanese potatoes aren't that great, but the corn is delicious. In some of the restaurants, in Tokyo, they import Idaho potatoes. I like the Idaho potatoes. I think they are the best in the world."

"Damn right! Everything in America is the best in the world," proclaimed Henry with pride.

Kenji smiled. Then he remembered the photographs above the fireplace.

"You know, in Japan, we don't display family pictures in the house. We display only the pictures of dead persons in big black and white photos leaning down on a high wall in a room where *butsudan* is displayed."

"What's the boots-dung?" asked Henry.

"It's a small household Buddhist shrine for praying. It

has candles, a water bowl, and a small rice bowl. But many people display books to impress people."

"Yeah, we got some Readers' Digest Condensed Books on display so people will think we're too busy to read the whole book," George said sarcastically.

"The Japanese really read a lot?" asked Mary.

"Yes, we do."

"Do you have family albums in Japan?"

"Yes. We keep our pictures in the albums."

"We have albums, too," said John. "May I see pictures of your family?"

"They are all in Japan."

"You don't carry pictures of your family?" asked Henry.

"Japanese people never carry photographs of their family," said Kenji. "I have just one...of my girlfriend."

"May I see?" said John

Kenji took the pocketbook out of his pocket, opened it, took out Inga's picture, and handed it to John.

"Wow, she's pretty!" he said.

George looked over at the photograph and let out a whistle of approval. John handed it down to his mother. She looked at it with Henry. Henry didn't say anything, but Mary commented, "She's very beautiful, Kenji."

When they passed the picture back to Kenji, he took one last look at her before putting it back.

"What does her father do?" asked Mary.

"He is a professor at Caltech in the Mathematics Department."

"What's Caltech?" asked Henry.

"California Institute of Technology. It's a very famous American university."

"I see," said Henry as he mopped the gravy off his plate.

After the large breakfast, it was time to go their separate ways for a rest. Kenji went upstairs and went into his room and wrote a letter to his father.

Dear father,

I know I couldn't please you as you wish. I have been trying hard to be the man that you have been wishing for.

Making the decision whether to marry her or not is emotional torture for me. I need more time to reach a decision.

As you know, I have only one year left to finish school. It would be a great tragedy for me if you don't send me the tuition.

Temporarily, I am staying on a farm in Nebraska, learning a new kind of work, and also a great deal about myself.

Your Son,
Kenji

After writing the letter, he took out one of the stamps from his pocketbook, applied it, went outside, put it into the mailbox, raised the red pole, and returned to the house.

As Kenji stepped into the living room, Mary said, "Kenji, why don't you come over here," She touched the sofa. "We have the family albums if you are interested."

"Oh, yes, I would like to see them," he said.

On the coffee table were four albums of hand-tooled leather with many black pages.

Kenji sat on the large white overstuffed sofa between Mary and John. Henry sat in an arm chair at the corner of the couch near Mary. George sat next to John.

Mary opened the top album. Inside were many brown tinted, grayish black and white and a few color photographs.

"Oh, look at this," said Mary, as she pointed to a black and white photograph of a young Henry holding a very chubby baby with white icing on the end of his nose. There was one candle on the center of the cake. "Here's George on his first birthday. He got so excited. He tried to crawl on the cake."

George strained toward the album to get a closer look. "Yeah. See how happy Dad is. Look at that smile. That's when he still liked me."

"Your father has always loved you," said Mary.

"Yeah, maybe. But he liked me a hell of a lot better back then."

Kenji looked over at Henry, who sat passively.

"Kenji, look here!" John yelled out, pointing at an extreme close-up of an anonymous palm of a hand, with a set of pink curlers and an eye barely visible between the fingers. "I took that picture. Mom was trying to perm her hair. I got her by surprise."

Kenji looked over a few more pages learning more about the Harris family. He noticed that Mike and John had received numerous awards. There were pictures of John winning a first place trophy for the rabbits that he had raised as a 4-H project and another one of John at the spelling bee county finals. Mike had numerous photographs of him winning trophies in baseball, football, and debate competitions. Another photograph showed him in his cap and gown as class valedictorian.

As Mary turned the page of the album, Kenji noticed a brown-tinted photograph of the three marines standing with arms over their shoulders smiling directly into the camera with the Wako Building in Tokyo in the background.

"I know that place," Kenji pointed to the picture. "That's in the Ginza, the most exclusive shopping district, in Tokyo. My family has the same picture."

George imitated some type of spooky movie music, "Oooo wooooo oooo oooo."

"Cut that out, George!" cried John.

"Don't scare your brother like that!" Mary said.

"My grandfather on my father's side had an antique shop in the Ginza but it was destroyed by the bombardment during the war," Kenji told them. "He was rich, very rich."

"Are you rich, too?" John asked.

"It's not polite to ask that kind of question." Mary scolded John. "He's my father-in-law." she said to Kenji, pointing at one of the three soldiers. "He was a marine during World War II."

"My grandfather, from my mother's side, was a soldier in World War II. He died in Manchuria," said Kenji.

"That's terrible, that people have to die in wars like that," said Mary, shaking her head in remorse.

Mary continued turning the pages. There were many covering Mike's travels in the Navy. In one picture he was dressed like a Maori warrior in New Zealand. He was wearing a Kiwi feather cloak, holding a spear, and had many lines of fake tattoo on his face. Mike's personality still penetrated through the make-up and he was recognizable. Another picture showed him standing in front of the statues of the elephants at the Grand Palace in Bangkok. In another was Mike in a motorized rickshaw with the driver. On the next page, Mike was posing with a pretty young Filipino woman in most of the photographs.

"Who is the young woman?" Kenji asked.

"That's Rosalinda, Mike's wife," answered Henry.

"Dad almost killed Mike when he found out she was from the Philippines," added George.

"Mike has a certain way about him. Nobody ever stays mad at him very long," explained Mary.

"He can charm the spots off a leopard," said George.

"What is that, charm the spots off a leopard?" said Kenji.

"I don't know how to explain it," George said.

"You see, Mike has one of those personalities that everybody likes. He's always had lots of friends. People are just naturally attracted to Mike," said Henry.

Kenji looked at the picture of Mike. It was a very nice face. Very friendly. He understood how someone could trust him easily.

"The day Mike and Rosalinda were supposed to arrive, Dad was storming around the house yelling that no son of his was going to bring a foreigner into his house," said George. "But within five minutes, Mike had Dad purring like a kitten."

Kenji wishfully thought to himself that maybe his father's attitude toward him and Inga might also change with a similar magic.

"Mike and his wife just had a son this year," Mary said, "Henry and I are very excited about seeing the baby when they come to visit this fall."

Henry's face glowed with pride, "We're anxious to see our first grandchild. I'm going to make a farmer out of him."

"Dad bought a baby-size set of bib-overalls and a little straw hat," said John.

"You can't start too young," added Henry.

Mary turned another page of the photo album.

"Is that George?" Kenji asked, pointing to a photograph of a young man leaping a hurdle. There was also another photograph of the young man receiving an award in track.

"No. That's Dad," said George.

"The resemblance is amazing," said Kenji.

"Yeah, isn't it?" said George in disgust.

"Listen here, boy, if you'd get your ass in gear maybe then you'd make something of yourself," argued Henry.

"Please, not in front of our guest," said Mary.

"That's George," said John, pointing out a color snapshot.

Kenji looked at a picture of George standing in front of an old tractor.

"See that tractor," said Henry. "George tried to fix the damn thing three years ago and its still sitting out there. It's a pile of rusting scrap iron now."

"Maybe if you'd give me a little encouragement, or talk to me instead of at me, I'd be as much of a success as your prima donna sons, Mike and John! But no! All you can do is criticize! You can never say anything nice to me. Just once! Just once!" With that last point made, George stood up and rushed out of the house.

Henry looked at his wife and she looked back at him. All of a sudden he burst out, saying, "Why are you looking at me that way? I didn't say a word." Then he got up and walked away.

Mary had a look of embarrassment on her face. "I'm really sorry that you had to see that," she told Kenji.

"Maybe I should talk with George," said Kenji.

"I don't know. George and Henry have been a little high-strung ever since Mike left for the Navy," said Mary.

Kenji got up, off the sofa, and walked out the front door to where the muffled sound of heavy-metal rock music could be heard emanating from George's car. The windows were rolled-up tight and George was playing intense musical licks on an air-guitar.

Kenji hesitated for a moment wondering if he should interrupt. Then he decided that George probably needed someone to talk to. He knocked on the closed window. George continued playing the imaginary instrument. Kenji knocked again louder. George looked up, turned the music off, and rolled down the window.

"Wha 'd ya want!" He yelled.

"I thought you might need someone to talk to."

George waited a few moments and then said, "O.K., get in."

Kenji walked around and then opened the passenger side door and entered.

In anger, George said, "You wanna talk? Talk!"

"Are you upset?"

"No, I'm in a great mood," George spat.

Kenji sat in the car without saying a word, feeling uncomfortable. He didn't know what to say.

Just as Kenji decided to leave, George stopped him.

"Wait a minute. I really appreciate the effort. What do you say we drive into town?"

"All right. That's a good idea."

George started the car, gunned the engine, and kicked up a large cloud of brown dust.

As the car approached U.S. route 281, George asked, "You like 'Twisted Sister'?"

"I don't know."

George let out a fiendish laugh and popped a tape in the cassette player. The music blasted through the car. Kenji could feel the inside door panels vibrating to the beat of the loud music and began wondering if it was a good idea to be in the car after what happened. George then turned the music down to a more comfortable level, although they both had to raise their voices somewhat to be heard.

"Sorry about that, but I couldn't resist," laughed George.

Kenji looked at George and said, "I prefer jazz."

"I've heard it. I guess it's O.K."

"Do you really not like your father?" asked Kenji.

"I don't like to say this, but sometimes I really hate the guy. But I respect him too. You know what I'm trying to say?"

"No."

George turned the music off.

"Remember how when we were looking at the photo album, that Mike, John, and my Dad all had pictures where they're posing with trophies and things like that?"

"Yes. You must feel very proud of them."

"Kinda, but did you also notice that there weren't any pictures of me with any kind of awards?"

"No, I didn't."

"Well, the reason is that Mike was good in school and John is good in school, but I wasn't. I've never been that smart in schoolwork. And you know what else?"

"What?"

"My Dad was offered a scholarship to go to college. But he turned it down. Can you believe that?"

"Why would he turn down a scholarship?"

"Because he's got this crazy idea that the world revolves around farming."

"Farming is important."

"Right. But my Dad is obsessed with it. You've been here long enough. You've seen it, haven't you? If you want to get on my Dad's good side, just get him to talk about farming. John knows how to stroke my Dad real good."

"Stroke?"

"Yeah, you know. Push his button. Tell him what he likes to hear."

"I see."

Downtown Grand Island was coming into view.

"I'm going to buy a pair of boots," said George. "Do you need anything?"

"Maybe I will buy a shirt and some new shoes."

"There's a place here where you can buy a good pair of work boots real cheap."

George parked the car and they both walked to a second-hand store.

"I don't like second-hand things," said Kenji.

"Well, then we can go to a K-mart. They have some good low-priced work boots."

"I prefer nice boots that have a leather sole."

"You don't want a leather sole. If you step on a cow patty with a leather sole, you'll end up flat on your ass."

"I never buy cheap things. I always buy quality merchandise, especially clothes and shoes."

"Hey, if you want nice boots, I'll take you later. But, I thought you said you were having financial problems."

"Maybe you're right." Kenji thought that he shouldn't spend his money.

In a second-hand store, George bought a pair of work

shoes.

On the way back to the car, George pointed out both the commercial and residential sides of the town. The houses and stores looked brand new. There were damaged and twisted trees that lined the streets and cut into the sky like black spikes. Several were dead. Others had just a few shiny fresh shoots on the trunk, battling to stay alive.

"What happened?" asked Kenji.

"Tornado."

"I've heard about tornadoes."

"This one hit two years ago and five people got killed."

"It must be very frightening," Kenji said as he looked closely at the damage. "In Japan, we don't have tornados. But we have typhoons. You know, strong winds and high water. It does bad damage, but not like this."

"When the tornado hits, it sounds like a train coming at you. It looks like a big black twisting cone and it's got trees torn out from the roots, pieces of houses, cars, whatever it can suck up into its funnel. You gotta watch out when the days get real hot, because that's when they hit."

Kenji looked up into the sky and saw some dark clouds on the horizon. He became nervous and turned to George.

"Let's get out of here, George."

Nine

By 10 A.M., Henry, John and Kenji were hooking up the red mobile long-range irrigation system behind the muddy John Deere tractor. It looked like a giant double decked yo-yo laying on its side. Kenji rapped a knuckle on the cartwheel-like reel of the giant yo-yo. It was solid steel. They all wore baseball caps, white T-shirts and blue jeans.

"Kenji, these are all my toys," Henry said proudly, pointing to the colorful farm machinery scattered around the farmyard.

"In your huge playground."

"Right," smiled Henry. Then, suddenly, he turned to George who was approaching. He also wore jeans but he wore a cowboy hat and a black tee-shirt with pictures on the front. "You don't wear a damn black shirt out here in this heat! It'll soak up the sun's rays!"

George said nothing.

You might think George wore that outfit simply because he wanted to upset his father.

"It's another scorching day," said John as he wiped the sweat from his brow with the back of his hand.

"Beautiful sky," said Kenji, looking up.

"You can never trust Nebraska sky," said George. "Look at the wall." He pointed to the many pockmarks above the windows of the house. "Those marks were made by hailstones these last three summers."

"They look like they've been struck by a low-flying jet fighter," said Kenji.

"Yeah, it's a real war when the hailstorms hit."

"The sky appears very calm," Kenji said.

"Unless you're a gambler, farming in Nebraska is for nothing if a strong hailstorm hits your crops."

"Shut up!" yelled Henry. "I don't want to hear nothing about no hailstorms!"

"Do you gamble, Kenji?" asked John, trying to change the subject.

"No, I don't."

Now they all climbed up to the tractor. Henry started the engine. Kenji sat close to John on the left fender while George sat on the right fender alone. Kenji felt the hot fender that had been heated by the sun.

Dragging the reels behind them, the tractor slowly made its way out to the cornfield. The tractor seemed to move by itself as if it knew the direction like a cow.

Passing by an old, beat-up tractor, resting on flat tires with worn off paint, its parts all over the ground surrounding it as if it had exploded, Henry shouted to George over the noise of the engine. "When you gonna finish fixing up that tractor?"

"I'll probably have it done this month," George shouted back.

"Make it run like a deer!" shouted Henry. "And don't forget to paint it the way I like it — red wheels and a green body!"

"Don't worry Dad. You know I can fix almost anything. It'll look good before I'm through with it," George replied. He seemed proud of his mechanical abilities.

"I hope so," his father answered.

"Kenji, do you know the meaning of Nebraska?" asked John.

"No."

"It means flat lands and flat rivers. It's a name given by the Indians."

"I think it's a very appropriate name," said Kenji, surveying the land.

As they approached the edge of the cornfield, Henry shouted joyfully, "Beautiful corn! Look at those ears! They're getting bigger and bigger!" Under the sharp sun, the rich dark green leaves were shinning oily and the green husks, tightly wrapping the ears, were growing to maturity.

"They're shooting up fast!" said John with enthusiasm.

"This is gonna be the best year we've ever had!" Henry's deep voice replied.

"Three years in a row you've said that and each year we lost to a stupid hailstorm!" George said, not without sarcasm. "One more time and the party's over!"

"Oh, shut up! You're too pessimistic!" Henry spat.

"I like the sweet smell of corn in the air," Kenji said, breathing deeply. "Good smell!"

Less impressed, and bored, George jumped off the tractor onto the soft dirt lane of the cornfield, and walked to a yellow tractor, which was parked with a water-gun traveller attached to the back of it.

George worked alone, unhooking the cable wire between the water-gun traveller and the tractor.

Henry, Kenji and John rode on ahead down the muddy lane on the first tractor. John had moved over to the other fender.

Kenji was looking back at George who was now climbing up onto the tractor. He started the engine, and swung the vehicle around, putting the water-gun traveller into a proper position. "He is performing beautifully."

"He knows what a farmer has to do," said John.

"He just doesn't like to do it," said Henry sarcastically.

On the dirt lane, there were many imprints left by the heavy tractor on the previous days. New imprints, as the tractor pushed forward down the lane, overlapped the old ones.

Grasshoppers frantically leaped out of the way of the tractor. One large green one leaped onto the tractor, landing atop the warm engine, where he remained like a hood ornament. Kenji and the grasshopper glared at each other for a few moments before the insect jumped off, making a fluttering sound with its yellow wings.

"That cloud looks like that modern sculpture that George made in school," Kenji pointed out.

"That one?" Henry pointed.

"No, that one," repointed Kenji.

"You mean that crazy thing in his room?"

"Yes."

Henry shook his head as they moved on. And, now, Henry stopped the tractor, put it in park, and they all climbed down.

The three of them started to set the irrigation as their boots all sank deeper into the muddy lane.

Henry pushed the throttle up and down, as Kenji and John were moving their hands busily — hooking and unhooking the heavy coupler of the rubber pipe, connecting and disconnecting the shaft frequently.

Now one of the reels began to turn slowly as Henry pushed the throttle up, accelerating the engine and its power, retrieving the collapsed rubber pipe heavily and tightly, like a typist reeling the ribbon in an empty typewriter reel, turning slowly.

The noisy repetitions of the engine crashed against the silence of the field. The only other noise Kenji noticed was coming from a small airplane flying high overhead, appearing and disappearing in the clouds as it cast its shadow on the cornfield.

After the rubber pipe was retrieved and wound tightly around the reel, Henry climbed up into the driver's seat and then John and Kenji each sat on the fenders, and the three of them began once again to move down the lane, pulling reels behind them.

Suddenly Kenji, sitting on the fender as he was cleaning mud off his boots, had a feeling of Nebraska farm life as if California and his college life were in another world.

In the distance, the tall exhaust pipe of George's tractor gave out smoke that appeared across the field, cutting through the sea of green corn stalks.

"Do we have to set irrigation every day?" asked Kenji.

"Every day," said Henry. "In this damn hot weather, you have to fight back!"

Reaching a dry lane, in the middle of the cornfield, Henry stopped as John jumped down from the tractor. John worked at the rubber pipe-reel, while Henry backed up.

"Got no choice! Crops can grow without a farm and without a farmer. But they can't grow without water! Water and the sun! They work in harmony. If you have lots of both, your crops grow straight and high and fast." Henry acted more like a teacher than an employer.

Henry and Kenji were heading to the irrigation-well while John was hooking the coupler of the end of the rubber pipe to the end of the irrigation-pipe and while George was pulling the greased release-cable from the water-gun traveller on his tractor along the dry dirt lane.

Reaching the irrigation-well, they both got down.

At the top of the well there was a big green motor. There was tall grass and the grass grew thick around the motor. There was an oily smell that clashed with the sweet scent of corn in the air.

Henry took a bunch of keys out of his pocket, selected one of them, started the engine while pressing the button on the motor. The engine noise shattered the silence in the field and the motor groaned as it strained to start bringing up water from the deep underground well.

"Kenji, look out!" Henry pointed out over the cornfield, as he was pushing the throttle forward accelerating the engine and its power.

In the far distance, above the corn stalks, a solid white

stream of water shot out against the clear blue sky, but it, then, fell gently and peacefully to earth.

"Beautiful!" Kenji said.

"It's a very powerful water-gun!" Henry said proudly, looking out at the solid white stream of water.

"Standing by that sophisticated motor you look like a good mechanic," said Kenji.

"Not like a dumb farmer?" asked Henry jokingly.

"Oh, no."

Henry leaned against a thick main iron pipe, that extended from the irrigation well beside the motor, and picked up the water spigot. He pushed it at the water tap, turning it a certain way, and suddenly a solid stream of cold water erupted from the opening. He bent down, as he took off his cap, and took a long drink right from the stream of water and then splashed the water over his face and head.

"Delicious, Kenji. Want some?" Henry asked, standing up as his right hand ran over his short gray hair making a sprinkle above his head.

"Sure," Kenji drank in the same way. He felt the cold and fresh water was running down slowly and coolly in his body. He also washed his face with the cold water. He felt good. "Icy cold!" He wiped his mouth with the back of his hand.

"You know, Kenji, this is the best, purest, and freshest water you'll ever taste because there are lots of pebbles along the underground well table. It comes from about one hundred fifty feet down. It's just the best."

"Do you ever run out of water?"

"No. They say there's enough water underneath the ground, in Nebraska, to flood our entire state to a depth of thirty-four feet. It's expensive to pump it up, but it's there for you if you need it."

"I see."

"Rain might be better and cheaper. But you can't depend on it all the time. Sometimes you don't get enough rain and

sometimes you get too much. Neither one is much help. Two
years ago, we had enough rain so we didn't have to irrigate
for the entire summer. That was one easy summer. But then
the corn was too short because there wasn't enough sun.
Thank God, we can always make it up with the water-gun if
we need to."

"So the underground water helps the farming a lot in
Nebraska?"

"You bet! I believe that the most successful crop production is only in the irrigated areas," said Henry confidently.
"'Course, once the hailstones hit, it didn't matter, anyway,"
he admitted. Then, all of a sudden, he looked sad.

Perhaps he reminded himself of what had happened the
last three summers, Kenji thought. So he tried to change the
subject. "Is a drought better than a flood?" he asked.

"Well, that's a helluva choice. But, it's a lot easier to add
water than to take it away."

Henry led Kenji into the deep corn field along a corn
row. Kenji felt his boots sink into deep, soft soil as he
walked. He touched a few growing stalks and could feel their
strength and resilience and felt their pinkish green shafts that
went deep into the earth.

Henry stopped and took a big ear of corn off a tall stalk.

"See, beautiful corn!" he said as he pulled away the husk
that tightly wrapped the ear and handed the naked ear to
Kenji.

Kenji brought it up to his nose and smelled it. "I'm going
to be drunk from the sweet aroma."

"Corn is the result of cross-fertilization. Tiny yellow single spores of pollen fall down on the silk by the wind. The
pollen grains are like males and the silks are like females,"
Henry became the teacher again.

"Sex in the corn field," said Kenji with a laugh.

Henry laughed even louder, arousing Kenji suspicion that
Henry might had sex in the corn field.

As they walked on, Henry kept repeating, over and over,

how great the corn would be this year.

He bent down and picked up a bit of soil and made a mud ball in his big hand as he walked. "Beautiful soil," he mumbled to himself.

Kenji also picked up some. The soil was rich, brown, and sandy. It was warm and soft like fine brown sugar. Then he was being kept busy trying to brush away mosquitoes.

"Where do all these mosquitoes come from?"

"This is a good breeding ground for them because the ground is always damp. They never seem to bother me. I don't think they like my blood very much. They may like Japanese blood."

They heard, as they neared the water-gun traveller, the sound of shi-shi-shi-shi-shi-shi-, spraying the water.

"It's raining here!" said Henry. He grinned.

They quickly ran over to the forceful water-gun traveller and stood right underneath it to avoid getting themselves wet. Everything was wet around the water-gun traveller and the rubber pipe swelled as it supplied water all the way up to the water-gun.

"Kenji, don't be stupid! If you were to put your hand at the gun point that water would take your hand right off," warned Henry as he pointed up.

As the water continued to shoot out across the field, the water-gun made a quick reverse move to go back to its original starting point, after it had made a full circle at regular speed, and then shi-shi-shi-shi-shi- as a heavy metal bar, at the gun point, hitting regularly and forcefully at the water stream as the water-gun traveller was moving very slowly like a snail, heading toward the other end of the lane where the yellow tractor was holding the greasy wire, as it was spraying and winding the greasy wire inside the drum.

"The water is coming this way," said Kenji.

"Let's get out of here," said Henry.

They hurriedly got into the row of corn stalks and walked away. Kenji turned and saw a huge rainbow in the sky, above the cornfield.

All in all, it had been an extraordinary experience for Kenji, not because he had seen new farming instruments and techniques, or because he had learned something of the weather and soil, or even something new about nature. No, in addition to all those things, this learning experience had taught Kenji a lot about himself.

At the root of it all, he had discovered a new curiosity within himself. He had also sensed a new realm of appreciations brewing deep within. Never before had he seen nature as both a killer and a provider, a villain and a protector, a teacher and a tester. Never before, indeed, had he seen himself as an explorer in a new land, able and ready to seize the day, ready to learn tirelessly, ready to travel as far as he could go. Just this outing today had inspired him to reach far and anew in the furtherance of his own life. And, oddly, this new inspiration was spelled N-E-B-R-A-S-K-A, and, thought Kenji, the Indians who named it could not have known in a million years of the grand and life-affirming effect that land would have upon him.

Ten

After lunch George took Kenji to Jack's garage. There, Kenji saw the Porsche. The engine compartment was empty and the engine itself lay in the garage, dissected and examined, like a patient about to undergo open heart surgery.

George was looking at the car like a child staring in a candy store window.

"You're a very lucky young man," the short-haired mechanic said to Kenji. "I checked it over. We need only a few parts for the engine."

Kenji seemed relieved. "How much will it cost?"

"I haven't got the exact estimate yet but probably around six-hundred or so, including the labor."

The price was much less than Kenji had expected, but he still felt down. He took out his wallet, looked through, and counted out the money he had on hand. There was eight-hundred and seventy dollars in traveller's checks and twenty-five dollars in cash. Kenji calculated that with the money coming from Henry and with what he already had, he should be able to continue his trip. He breathed a sigh of relief.

"How long will it take?"

"Anywhere from one to three weeks. It all depends on how soon I can get the parts."

"Hey, Kenji, when you get this car fixed, do you think I could take it out for a spin?" asked George.

"It's not my car, George."

Kenji walked over to the telephone booth and called Inga.

"Hello," she said musically.

"Hi. This is Kenji."

"Oh, Kenji. Are you calling from New York?"

"No. I had some car trouble. I'm staying on a farm in Nebraska while the car is being repaired."

"How long do you think you'll be there?"

"Maybe a couple of weeks."

"Do you have enough money with you to fix the car?"

"I have part of the money to pay for the car's repairs if I don't spend frivolously. I'll also be making some money on the farm. By the way, Inga, I'm having a problem with my father."

"What kind of a problem?"

"He doesn't like the idea of us being involved. I may have to drop school and go back to Japan."

"I don't understand. What about your studies? This is your last year."

"I have no choice. My father won't send me any more money unless we stop seeing each other. He wants me to marry a Japanese girl after I've finished school. He says it will bring shame to the family if I marry you."

"That's terrible."

"I know. He's very stubborn. If I don't pay for next year's tuition, I'll have to drop out of school and then I'll lose my student visa."

"That's bad. If he's threatening to stop paying for your tuition, I'll quit school and work so you can finish your last year. It's no problem for me."

Kenji thought Inga was the most unselfish woman he had ever met and he was glad she loved him, but he didn't want to take away her education.

"I appreciate you for that, Inga. But I don't want you to

drop out of school. Even for a year."

"But I really do want to help you."

"Maybe I should go back to Japan. I'm sure I can change his mind."

"Don't worry about the tuition. We'll talk about that when you come back. I love you."

"I love you, too."

"I wish you good luck with your car and keep me informed about what's going on, Kenji."

"I will. Bye."

Kenji hung up the phone and got into George's car.

Returning from the town, they descended the stairs into the cool basement to have a game of pool. A large green pool table stood in the middle of the room where three large freezers were lined up against the wall.

George cheerfully grabbed a pool cue. Then he saw John, "Hey, get outta here, squirt!"

John turned red. "Shut up! Big mouth!" He stood for a moment, then walked up and out of the basement.

"For the rest of his life, he's gonna be on this damn farm but not me. I'm getting out of here as soon as I can."

"Where do you plan to go?" Kenji asked, chalking the tip of his cue.

"Anywhere people don't talk about farming."

"Would you like to join the Navy, like Mike?"

"I've taken just about all the orders that I can stand, so forget the Navy," said George. He racked up the balls.

Kenji broke them."You know, Kenji, I wouldn't mind going to..." George took a shot as he talked, pocketing a ball, "... California. I bet there's plenty of good surfing there, right?"

"Right. Especially in Malibu beach." Kenji had to watch his mouth now because Henry had ordered him not to speak to his son about California. He paused, then added. "You know, your father doesn't want me to say anything about

California to you."

"That figures. Damn him! I know he's afraid that I'm going to leave here."

"I had the same problem with my father, George. He didn't want me to go to America. But, I just insisted."

"I should leave without a word. But since Mike left, well, I guess it wouldn't be fair for me to take off and leave my Dad holding the bag. But if you were to stay..."

"But I have no experience. And I'm only temporary."

"I know. But I'll be shoving out of here one day. Believe me. Anything is better than working in this hell hole. You'll find out."

"I hope not."

"Kenji, do you think you'll get some money from Japan?"

"Possibly. Possibly not."

"Just in case you don't, why don't you stay here longer?"

"I will see. I have my own plan to carry out."

"So what about Inga? Are you going to marry her?"

"I don't know. But I love her. And not seeing her ever again will make me feel as if I am dead."

"Well, why don't you just marry her, then?"

"Because my father strongly disapproves of her."

"Has he ever met her?"

"No. He has never left Japan."

"He sounds like a real jerk to me."

"No. He's just a traditional man."

"My father doesn't like the town girls, but that's not about to stop me from seeing or marrying Lisa. And he knows it. You know, Kenji, I think you should take a firm stand on this and fight against your father's old traditions. You should show your father you can make your own decisions."

"But I don't want to lose the respect of my family."

To that, George had no reply. And suddenly, Kenji realized that respect in Japan and respect in America were two different things. George worked for his father, and did everything his father asked of him, and even understood his father to some degree, but he no longer respected him. The respect he had once felt had suffered diminution because of the way his father used him. On many occasions, George had complained, "My father sees me as a day-laborer, nothing more." On the other hand, Kenji's father had always been monetarily supportive without asking anything in return except for Kenji's loyalty to tradition.

That was it! Kenji's father, like all Japanese men were the same, respected tradition above all else — even family. Kenji even suspected his father didn't feel or understand the concept of love. Not of his wife, not of his sons. But he certainly had a deep and abiding love of tradition. George's father, on the other hand, reserved his respect first for the land, next for the idea of farming, or more precisely, dairying, and, somewhere down the line, the love of his family.

The difference in the two fathers, concluded Kenji in his private thoughts, centered about this pivotal and highly evocative word — respect. To the one father, the word bespoke the traditional heritage of an entire society. To the other, it meant, above all else, a shovelful of dirt. And who could possibly say the one father had a better sense of right or wrong, or of value, than the other.

Whether he should go back to Japan after finishing his education in America or stay in America wasn't known to Kenji. Just the thought of not seeing Inga anymore make him feel desperately lonely.

After the break, in the afternoon, they all returned to their chores; Kenji was cleaning the barn while George was working on the old tractor. John was cleaning the calf pen and Henry was chopping several rows of cornstalks to feed the cows. Mary, of course, was making up the rooms.

At about four in the afternoon they started the second

milking of the day and after the milking they all walked toward the farmhouse.

"Kenji, I've been meaning to apologize for calling your father a jerk."

"Don't apologize. He may be just that."

Eleven

Kenji, George and John were milking the cows in the barn in the early morning, but Mary and Henry still had not joined them. The loud Rock 'N' Roll blared out from the radio.

"Kenji, are you all right?" John asked. Kenji was staring into space.

"Yes, I was just thinking."

"Thinking of what? About Inga?"

"No. I was thinking about my family back in Japan."

Now Mary came into the barn to work and then, a bit later, the music suddenly changed from rock and roll to country. Henry had entered.

Again Henry was angry with George. But George, again this morning, did not talk back, keeping quietly to his milking chores.

As they finished the morning milk, George and Kenji were cleaning the back barn under the glare of a bare bulb.

Kenji really hated cleaning the back barn because of the strong stench. But he had no choice.

In frustration, he felt as if he was a prisoner laboring in a prison camp because he couldn't move on as he had originally scheduled. You might think George would have had the same feelings as Kenji because of the responsibilities he had hanging over him.

Finally the hard work had eased Kenji's frustration. The

hard work had made their white T-shirts soak up their sweat
so that the shirts now clung to their bodies.

Henry operated the tractor busily and skillfully, gathering the materials which were pitched out from the back barn.
Putting the tractor in gear Henry drove back and forth, oper-
ating the shifts of the huge front loader, grading the ground
to gather a scoopful of the cow's manure, lifting it, carrying
it to the manure-spreader of John's tractor, opening the
shovel, and dropping it in deftly. A big yellow butterfly sat
on a big piece of dried manure in the corral momentarily and
flew away pleasantly. Henry shoveled the waste and
dropped it into the manure-spreader continuously. The
sounds of the tractor's engine and the grinding steel of its
gears surrounded the peaceful early morning with noise as if
the noise were saying that another day of hard-work had
begun and it was a new day on a farm. John, on his tractor,
pulled the manure-spreader toward the empty cornfield to
spread the waste out as fertilizer to make the soil fertile for
the next year's growing season. It would have been easy for
a cornfield philosopher to conclude that the singular spring-
time beauty of the field was somehow an end-product of
cow manure. Not because of plant growth and soil tilling.
But because manure itself was a direct expression of fine
and finished art.

Sweating and filthy from the morning's chores, they
washed and had breakfast.

Twelve

While they were enjoying lunch, John shouted pointing out through the window to the several pigs in the yard. "A hog is loose!"

At the news Henry was distracted, jumping up from his chair smashing his glass of water on the table. "Damn you, George! Why did you let the pigs out?"

"Are you crazy?" screamed George back at him. "I didn't let 'em out — they broke out!"

"Bullshit! That's why you came in late," said Henry. "Everybody out in the fields to round them up! Move!"

Henry didn't seem to believe George, but whose fault it was could be determined later. The most important thing now was to catch the pigs.

Kenji ran outside with the others, realizing that farm life would not be as easy or as predictable as he had imagined.

Kenji was surprised at how quickly and efficiently the Harris family moved into action during a crisis. They have obviously been through situations like this before, Kenji thought. That did not mean that Henry, whose face was flushed red with anger, was any calmer about it. But everyone seemed to know what to do. Within minutes, the entire family was out in the fields, chasing down loose pigs. Henry was giving out orders to his obedient troops like a general during a battle.

"John, you and George over to that side. Kenji, you come with me," commanded Henry as he took off down the dirt drive way. Kenji was surprised. For a man of his size and age, Henry was rather fast. Kenji could hardly keep up with him.

"One's headin' out to the highway," shouted Henry back to Kenji. "That's Old Smokey. He probably busted the fence and started this whole mess." Kenji saw a large, gray, rock-like thing ahead in the distance.

"There he is!" called Henry.

Henry waited for Kenji to catch up, and then the two of them slowly moved closer to the pig.

"Now what I want you to do is race by Old Smokey about ten yards. Then start whooping and jumping up and down. Scare the hell out of him. When he stops short, I'll grab him. Be careful that he doesn't run you down, though."

Kenji nodded his head in agreement and then sprinted by the pig who appeared to look more like a hippopotamus than a farm animal. Ten steps past the pig. Kenji stopped and started jumping up and down. He was shouting in Japanese at the pig: "*Buta yaro* (You fat pig)!" So that Henry could not understand nor Old Smokey. Old Smokey froze in his tracks, which allowed Henry to jump on its back and grab it by the ears. Old Smokey, having fallen for the Japanese-insult-in-cornfield-trick, kicked viciously with his back feet, but only swatted at empty air.

"The only way to hold a pig," advised Henry by way of demonstration, "is to grab it by the ears. You don't have to twist too hard. Because they're pretty damn sensitive."

Old Smokey snorted in anger, making Kenji feel glad that he was not the one doing the twisting of ears.

"Do you think John and George have the other pig by now?" asked Kenji.

"They better have a couple of them suckers by now. Pigs can tear up a cornfield. We gotta get the rest of them."

"How many are there?"

"Seven." Henry started to guide Old Smokey back to its pen. "I'll get him back where he belongs, and repair the damage."

A bulky figure darted past them a couple rows over.

"There goes another one, Kenji! Go get him — and don't forget to grab 'm by the ears!"

Kenji did as he was told. He noticed two things right away about this pig: it was neither as fat nor as slow as Old Smokey. As soon as Kenji got close to it, it took off like a sprinter in the Olympic games — right through the middle of the cornfield. Henry had made it all sound so simple. Just run by, jump on the back, twist the ears — presto! All done. But Kenji saw several problems here. First of all, the pig was very fast. More importantly, it looked a lot meaner than Old Smokey. Kenji tried to do as he was told, but the row was too narrow for him to pass the pig. Figuring out an alternative course of action, Kenji decided that he must pass the pig on the next row, then lie in wait behind some stalk and jump on it as it passed by. The best-laid plans — Kenji stuck his hand out to grab the pig, but its snout hit his hand, painfully knocking it out of the way. The pig then took off in another direction, cutting across the corn field, knocking down the growing stalks of green as if they were so many blades of grass being cut by a lawn mower. Kenji had visions of this pig destroying Henry's entire corn field before it was caught, and Kenji being to blame. I have to catch this pig before he ruins the cornfield, Kenji thought. He chased it into a long row where, at least, the pig didn't knock down any more cornstalks. But if its snout could hurt his hand, then Kenji had to be very careful of its cleft hooves. Sweat bathed Kenji, as if he were in a hot, dirty bath, and his breath came in heaving gasps. But, then, the pig's did too. It wasn't used to running, either.

Kenji ran parallel to the pig. If I could jump on its big round back, I could ride it for a moment until I hold of his ears, he thought to himself. Then the pig would stop. That seemed easy enough. He sprinted ahead several yards and vaulted onto the pig's broad gray back. So far, so good. But Kenji wasn't holding on with his feet. He was holding on with his stomach. And his hands weren't on the pig's head, but on its back. He had to swing himself around.

Finally, Kenji felt he was gaining control of the situation — which would have been news to the pig, who continued to romp down the row between the growing cornstalks unimpeded by its rider. Kenji finally hoisted himself onto the pig's back. And then, suddenly, it all became fun. Kenji had never ridden a horse but he imagined it must be something like this. The cornstalks continued to whiz past and the pig continued at full throttle. Kenji felt the animal's flesh beneath his jeans and he understood why people loved to ride horses. But he had to get this animal to stop. He leaned over the pig and grabbed hold of its right ear. He twisted firmly. The pig grunted and squealed. The pig, predictably, came to a stop. Kenji did not.

Kenji was on the ground and the pig was squealing and running off in the distance. Just then, there was a sharp crack! The cracking sound occurred once again. It sounded like gunshots, or a car back firing, only louder and more frightening. Kenji kept his nose in the dirt. He was thinking that he had been shot and was now dying. It seemed so strange that he had left Japan only to die on a Nebraska cornfield. His mother was right about the dangers in America. The left side of his head hurt. He checked it with his hand. There was blood!! Had he been shot in the head?

He touched the wound again. There was blood, but no hole, no deep wound. Another crack! He buried his head in the soil. He felt something run over his body. It was not a pig...too small for that. Nor was it not human...too small for that too. He opened his eyes and lifted his head. He almost afraid to look.

He was staring into the deep, probing eyes of one of the farm cats. The cat was purring as if it wanted to play.

"Can't you see I've been shot?" Kenji asked the cat.

The cat seemed not terribly impressed by his death scene.

Kenji touched the side of his head again with his hand. The hand came back with a little blood again. Was it possible that he hadn't been shot at all? He sat up, and looked around. No blood on the ground, no blood on the shoulders. His hand was a bit pained, but otherwise it was normal. You know what, Kenji? asked himself. You just scraped your head against a cornstalk. He laughed at how overly dramatic he had acted. But who had fired those shots? What for? He had to find out. And he was not doing his job, catching that pig.

Kenji slowly got up and started to walk toward the general area from which the shots came. Because of the ambient heat the sweat began pouring off his body. He heard the voice of John and George but couldn't make out what they were saying until he was only two rows from them. He heard George's voice.

"I can't believe you shot her, John."

"I didn't mean it. Beside, you gave me the gun."

"Don't blame it on me, you squirt. I was just trying to scare her back toward the pen."

"Don't tell Dad," John begged in a teary voice. "Please don't tell him. I'll bury Esmeralda. And we can say we didn't see her."

"Who the hell would believe a dumb story like that?"

Kenji saw what had happened as he came up to the boys standing above a fat, big gray pig that was lying in the field.

"Then what do you think I should do, George?" John, who held a handgun in his hand, asked. "Dad'll be so mad."

"It's just what you deserve, you little brown nose."

"Come on, George, let's bury her. Quick, before Dad comes back."

"You can't bury a pig!" said George. Then he looked up to see Kenji approaching and said, almost with pride,

"Kenji, look what John did."

Kenji looked at the pig, stretched out next to them on the ground. Its bloody snout made Kenji feel sad. He hated to see animals mistreated. And he suddenly felt like an authority figure to these two boys, neither of whom understood how wrong they were. "You're lucky only a pig was killed, guys." He told them. "You should know better than to play with guns."

"Save the lecture," said George scornfully, not about to take a lecture from someone who's been a farmer for only four days. "We're both gonna get it from Dad."

John seemed desperate. "Kenji, would you help me bury it?"

Kenji still felt to be the voice of wisdom. "No, what's happened is bad enough. It won't go away if you hide it. Are there any other pigs loose? I know there's at least one more. Let's catch it. Then tell your father. Things could be worse."

"That's what you think," said George.

Kenji heard a grunt and saw the pig he had been chasing a few rows away. For a moment, he was afraid the animal was going to charge and attack them in revenge for Esmeralda. But he realized that only happened in movies, not in real life. "Come on," Kenji said. "What's done is done. Nothing we can do about it now, except catch this other pig."

"Damn pigs!" George cursed. "I wish I had never seen a pig in my whole life."

"Me too!" said John. "Pretty soon I'm gonna be as dead as this pig."

"Su-ey! Su-ey!" George called, chasing after the pig. "Su-ey! Su-ey!"

They rounded up the last errant animal in a few minutes. George held it by the ears. They went down a row and out of the cornfield. Kenji could see the farmhouse, white and beautiful against the blue sky and the green trees, standing in the distance. They were walking slowly toward it; John was hanging back, clearly afraid to approach his father. When they came around a corner of the barn, Henry was leaning over the pigs who were grovelling in the mud and looking very happy and relaxed, in the pen, as if they had just had an interesting activity period. Henry turned to them.

"Only one?" There was supposed to be two coming back with Kenji and the two younger boys. "Where's Esmeralda?"

"I don't know..." John said quickly...too quickly. George looked at him as if to call him a coward or liar.

"John knows where Essie is," George said. "Tell him, John."

John looked as white as the clouds that passed overhead.

"Dad..." John began. "...uh..." He couldn't continue.

"What is it, son?" (Son always meant John. Henry loved John more than anything in the world, except for his farm.) Henry looked concerned, in a fatherly way. Kenji was glad he spoke gently.

"I...uh...I..."

"Jesus Christ!" George couldn't stand it any longer. "John shot Esmeralda with my gun! She's dead, back in the cornfield."

Kenji watched Henry's face. As the color of the older man's face darkened to a purplish-red, the nervous tension in Kenji also raised. He couldn't move and watched in horror as Henry's emotions flew directly at the small, frail John.

"What? You what?" Henry shouted. His fatherly concern quickly gave way to anger.

"I shot Esmeralda," John confessed. He started crying.

"How the hell...how the hell did you do that? What the hell were you doing with a gun?"

George spoke up, a little less certain this time. "I...uh...I took it out to scare the pigs."

"So...you're the one who's to blame," Henry turned on George.

"No, he's not," interrupted John. "I shot the pig. I don't

know why, either."

"That porker could have been worth two hundred dollars this time next year. Now I'll be lucky to get one hundred for her. George, you owe me one hundred."

"Why me?"

"For being stupid! That's why!"

"No, Dad," said John, slowly and deliberately, "I owe you the money. I've got over a hundred dollars saved. I'll even get a job in town."

"George can sell his car," said Henry, making it sound non negotiable.

"No way! I'm not selling my car for nothing!"

"Yes, you will," replied Henry, almost enjoying the contest of wills.

Mary appeared from the house. "What are you fighting about?"

"I shot Esmeralda," said John matter-of-factly.

"Oh, my God!"

"I'm leaving," said George. "Have a nice life."

"Where do you think you're going?"

"Anywhere that's away from here."

"You're not going anywhere!" Mary was tougher than Henry when she had to be. She was shocked at both Henry and George for their behavior. "Now," she said with a calming voice, "I don't know who shot Esmeralda. And, at this point, I don't care. What's done is done. And I'm not going to see our family break up over it. It's only money. We'll get it back somehow, like we always do."

"Two hundred dollars," groaned Henry.

"I wouldn't care if it was fifteen thousand, Henry. You only have three sons."

"Two," said Henry, with a glare toward George.

"See?" said George. "He hates me."

"Henry, you apologize to George," Mary was adamant.

"Mary, you keep quiet!"

Mary looked as if she was ready to explode. "Don't you

ever talk to me that way. I'm not one of your sons!"

"Dammit, then don't try to tell me what to do."

"John, George, and...Kenji...all of you, go back in the house and clean up again for lunch," commanded Mary, sounding as if she was getting ready to tear into Henry.

Kenji was upset. He hated family arguments.

George spoke up, as if felt the same way about family arguments. "If you really want me to, I'll sell my car to pay for the lost money on the pig."

"Just get in the house," said Mary, her voice still severe. George, John and Kenji all did as they were told. Kenji felt as though he was in a funeral procession.

George went up the stairs, punctuating his anger with a door slam. John went into the bathroom, while Kenji waited outside the door for his turn. He could hear Henry and Mary arguing outside, and he felt as though he was intruding in their family affairs.

He waited for John to come out of the bathroom. After a couple minutes of waiting, he heard a loud thump from inside, as if something fell on the floor.

"John!" he called out. "Hey, John, open up!"

There was no answer.

Kenji took out his pocket knife, pushed the awl into the hole in the bathroom knob, released the latch, opened the door, and saw John sprawled on the floor. He shouted to others as he knelt down beside him and felt his pulse. John was breathing evenly and he looked O.K. The strain and guilt of shooting Esmeralda had been too much for him. Kenji stretched him out comfortably on the floor, took a washcloth, wet it with cold water, and applied it to John's forehead. Footsteps approached the door.

"What's going...? John!!!" Henry rushed into the bathroom, kneeling down next to his son. "John...come on, son...John." He patted John's hand.

"He must have fainted," said Kenji. "I think we should get him to his room."

Henry was suddenly very somber. First, his wife had shouted at him, and now his favorite son had fainted. All because of him. "I shouldn't have yelled at him like that. John, I'm sorry. Please, John." He looked up in desperation. He called out into the hall. "Mary!!"

Mary came, running down the hall to the bathroom, wiping her hands on her apron. She said nothing as she almost leaped to John's side, kneeling down on the spotless linoleum floor next to him.

Now John's eyelids flickered. He looked up at everyone, except George, with half-closed eyes. "I'm sorry...I didn't mean to shoot Esmeral..."

"Never mind about that old sow!" muttered Henry. "What happened to you?"

"I don't know, Dad. One moment I was washing my hands, and the next moment, I'm down here on the floor."

Henry made a move to lift him, "Mother, let's carry him to his room."

"No, no, I'm all right," protested John, struggling to his feet.

"What he needs is food," said Mary, relieved that the crisis was over. "We all need some food."

Henry put his arm around John's shoulders and helped him out of the bathroom.

Kenji wondered where George was. So did Mary, and she called out his name.

"He's probably listening to that damn music of his," said Henry over his shoulder. Kenji knew that the crisis was officially over—Henry was back to complaining about George again. "The damn house could fall down and he wouldn't notice its collapsing. Kenji, go up and get George."

"No, I'll go," said Mary.

"Let Kenji go, woman. You get out in the kitchen and prepare the lunch."

Henry was very good at giving orders and everyone else was very good at following them.

Kenji knocked on George's door several times. There was no answer. Envisioning another member of the Harris family collapsed on the floor, Kenji burst into the room. George hardly bothered to look. Henry was right. When George was listening to his music nothing else seemed to matter. His earphones attaching him to the stereo like an astronaut's life line attached him to a space ship. George stood in the middle of the room where many posters of cars and rock stars were pasted on the walls, in a macho pose playing an imaginary guitar to the music only he could hear. And that was all he could hear.

"Let's finish the lunch," said Kenji.

George smiled, as if Kenji had just wished him a good day, and continued playing his imaginary guitar.

Kenji tried again with no more luck than before. He then realized the problem and started to pantomime an eating motion. George quickly understood, nodded, and then held up a finger to indicate he was just about finished. He then went into a very involved guitar ending to the song, paused a moment for applause from his imaginary audience, and then threw the earphones aside.

"Let's eat! I'm starved. I could eat Esmeralda." He took off down the stairs, Kenji trailing behind.

"John fainted in the bathroom," Kenji said to him.

"Serves him right, the little twerp."

"He's all right now, though."

George was unimpressed and said nothing.

After lunch, Kenji tried to call his parents but he couldn't get through. In frustration he went to his room and lay on the bed taking a nap and he had a dream that he was playfully walking with Inga in their bare feet holding their shoes in their hands on the sunbaked sand of Santa Monica Beach.

Once again, Kenji had occasion to compare the farm life culture of the Americans to the home he had read about in

boyhood in Japan. But this was not so much a comparison of
Henry to Kenji's father as it was a comparison of a well-
spring of reactions of an entire family to an emergency.
Actually, the emergency had occurred within a tightly cir-
cumscribed circle of financial concern — the market value
of a dead sow — but the bottom line was reached when
Henry's wife entered the equation. Kenji witnessed with his
own eyes and ears that once provoked to a certain degree,
Henry's wife had the last word.

And try as he might, Kenji could recall no instance in his
own home back in Japan where his father had ever been
openly tested — or yet screamed at — by his wife. Kenji's
mother, like most of all Japanese women, kept holding down
her emotions mostly in any circumstances. Slowly, but surely, Kenji was coming to understand clearly the difference
between a matriarchal and patriarchal society.

Stated succinctly, Henry's wife had accomplished in one
fit of discomfiture what few women — if any — had ever
accomplished in Japan.

Thirteen

The barn filled with country music as the cows were let in to be milked for the second time that day.

"You know," said Henry, now a nostalgic, "this barn was a playground when I was a kid. A lot of memories here. I used to catch mice up in the hayloft and keep 'em in a cage out back."

Kenji enjoyed hearing about the childhood of Henry Harris.

"My favorite time was the winter," Henry continued. "The barn would be warm because of all the cows. It was a great place for playing hide-and-seek with my brothers."

"How many brothers do you have?" asked Kenji.

"Two. The oldest one died in the Korean War. His name was Bill, and he was ten years older than me. The other older brother, Jim, lives in Vermont. He used to work for the Post Office, but he's retired now. He tills a little backyard garden."

"He went up to see him one year ago," said Mary, "and we couldn't believe how big his vegetables were. Twice as big as ours...right, John?"

"Yeah, Uncle Jim grows tomatoes twice as big as my head."

"That's a bit of an exaggeration," chided Mary, "but they were very large."

"How does he do that?" asked Kenji.

"Witchcraft," said Henry.

"No, it's not witchcraft," said Mary with some impatience, as if she and Henry had gone the rounds with this particular discussion many times before. "It's called the Findhorn Method. That's the name of a group of people in England who grow huge vegetables by talking to them and saying incantations over them. They felt that everything on this earth has soul. So, if they want a big tomato or watermelon, they appeal to its soul."

Henry obviously had no interest in this discussion at all. He was only too happy to change the subject.

"Here comes a Japanese cow. Come here, Elizabeth. Come here." Henry was speaking to a little cow as Kenji let her in through the half-door. Kenji could understand right away why Henry said she was Japanese. She was small with a few white spots dappled over her brown body; she was the odd brown one. She looked shy with a friendly face with big brown eyes. "Please come here, Elizabeth," said Henry. "I want to talk to your soul."

"She's the youngest and smallest of our full-grown cows," explained Mary.

"I saw her soul as Kenji let her in the door." He put his face next to the cow and whispered to her. "We need a lot of milk from you, Elizabeth. Won't you grow up to be big and fat and filled with milk the way all your relatives are? Can't you do that for us?"

"That's not exactly how your brother does it when he talks to his plants, Henry," said Mary, in a good-humored way.

"It's close enough," protested Henry. He patted the little cow on the rump and she hurried into a milking stall.

"You know, her mother died a few years ago," said Mary sadly.

"That's right. She cut herself badly up on some barbed wire and we couldn't stop the bleeding. Flies started attacking the wound and it became infected. Finally we had to shoot her to put her out of her misery." Henry shook his head.

"How terrible!" said Kenji.

"You bet," Henry said. "You know how she got hurt? Some town boys threw rocks at her and then they ran through the field close to the barbed wire fence. Cows run when strangers run and they get angry just like humans do."

Henry was now becoming angry.

"We're not positive that's how it happened," said George, trying to calm down his father, "but..."

"No, we're not sure," interrupted Henry, with a sarcastic tone of voice. "We only saw their footprints and watched them get in their car and drive away. They were probably some of your friends, George." Henry gave George a dirty look.

"Come on, you two," soothed Mary, "that was two summers ago."

Everyone seemed to agree to forget the subject. What impressed Kenji was that, while they were talking, none of the Harris family had lost the rhythm of the milking procedure.

John was rubbing the cow's udders gently to help to get all of the milk from them as he knelt down on the straw-covered dirt ground. After looking into the glass jar to make sure no milk still flowed from the cow, he detached the milk cups, one by one, from the now dry udders. They came off with a loud sucking noise that sounded like water being sucked down a drain. John attached them to the waiting cow in the next stall. Then Mary took off the leather strap and chain and pulled a long metal pin releasing the animal.

Opening the half-door, Kenji allowed another cow in. She rushed in and got into an empty stall and an unexpected one quickly followed before Kenji could shut the door. Since there wasn't a vacant stall, she tried to return to the back barn but became nervous when she saw Kenji standing by the half door. She panicked momentarily but Kenji managed to get her back into the back barn.

"Kenji, now you have been around cows for a couple days. How do you like them?" asked Henry, taking off the pin, as he freed a cow into the corral.

"Yes, I like them. I like their big honest eyes and friendly faces," replied Kenji, sending in a new cow.

"But you better watch out," Mary warned. "Though they have friendly faces some cows are not friendly."

Kenji smiled.

"You know, Kenji, I like them all, even the bad tempered ones. Because they're all like my daughters," said Henry.

"You're a happy man because your daughters make you rich," said Kenji, jokingly.

"You bet," Henry said. "That's why I like them."

"Send in another one, Kenji," said John.

"You didn't milk that one yet," said Kenji. "Why do you want another?"

"Because this one doesn't have enough milk."

As Kenji opened the half-door, a cow suddenly stepped back a little bit when she saw Kenji and studied Kenji's eyes suspiciously. So Kenji quickly hid himself at the side of the door. "Oh, come on in my friend." Kenji said in his mind. Then she slowly came in and hurried to an empty stall near the half-door.

"Look! This cow is carrying the Japanese map on her body. You see. This is Hokkaido. This is long Honshu. This is Shikoku. Oh, one island, Kyushu, is missing," said Kenji. He pointed to the black spots on the side of the cow. Then he turned around to the other side of the cow. "Oh, right here is Kyushu. But it doesn't look similar. But it's O.K." Then he turned around again. "Here, in Hokkaido, there are many dairy farms. It's an agricultural island."

"Where is Tokyo, where you came from?" asked Mary.

"Right here," Kenji pointed. "And Mount Fuji is just

right here. Not far from Tokyo. You can see it even from Tokyo when the weather is good. It's the highest mountain in Japan and it's also the symbol of Japan to many people."

"I know it's a beautiful mountain," said Mary, releasing a cow to the corral after milking it.

Kenji sent in another cow.

"Kenji, just remember that cow. She is extremely nervous and she has a quick temper," said Mary pointing to the cow which now came in. "She once kicked George's leg and broke it."

"Do they kick like a horse?"

"Yes, they do."

George did not talk much as the country music played, filling the barn with its melancholy twang.

Now Kenji went to the back barn. When he opened the large sliding door, this time, he felt at one with the surroundings. The blue of the sky, the bright sunshine, the green of the growing corn, the peaceful, contented cows, quietly awaiting their turns, some of them leaning their heads on the back of others. Kenji felt that he was a part of all this. He belonged.

"Kenji! Get the hell over here and send in more cows!" commanded Henry, like a dictator. Perhaps Henry only became coarse and demanding with those he knew well. Everything else was comfortable, but Henry was definitely abrasive. Oddly, Kenji could understand why Henry acted the way he did. A farm, which has been very unlucky despite having difficulty managing today's farm business, probably needed a forceful personality such as Henry's. Farms were not, and could not be, democracies. They needed benevolent dictators like Henry. Kenji realized all of this. But he was still not completely comfortable with it.

Kenji let ten cows in and then shut the door, and returned to the milk barn and allowed a cow to go into an empty stall.

"Kenji, how do you say cow in Japanese?" Henry asked.

"Ushi."

They all pronounced it, except George.

"But the same word means both a cow or a bull."

"Very interesting," said Mary.

"Send another ushi," said Henry.

Mary smiled.

Just at that same time, George screamed, "You bitch!" He punched a cow's chest brutally with his fist and then quickly took out an extra leather strap for milking from the wall and slapped her with it fiercely across her body. But she was calm and stood like a big rock. Kenji felt sad because he loved the animals.

"Stop it! Stop it! Stop it!" shouted Henry, as the vein bulged out from his forehead, running over to the middle of the barn where George was working. "Don't ever do that again!" he warned George, shaking a finger at him.

"That stupid cow stepped on my foot!" George said angrily. He started to limp around the barn.

"It's not her fault. If you had not been day dreaming it wouldn't have happened," said Henry.

"Be careful around them, Kenji. They're bigger and stronger than we are. They could hurt you without even knowing it. George looks O.K. But you could lose the feeling for a month if a cow stepped on your toe," Mary advised.

"I wonder what would happen if an elephant stepped on your toe," said Kenji.

"You could lose the feeling for a year," said Mary.

Once the crisis with George's foot was over, George was back doing what he had finished.

Kenji watched John injecting a liquid called Anavodic into the big teats of a cow; as the needle was pushed into the udder, the cow seemed used to it and reacted not at all.

John had explained it was to take the swelling out of hardened udders. After he emptied the plastic syringe into them, he massaged them gently.

"John is very good with animals. Often he has helped to deliver calves. He has a special talent," Mary said.

"Why don't you become a veterinarian, John?" Kenji's question was innocent enough but it struck a wrong chord with Henry.

"Hummf!" growled Henry. "One thing this world doesn't need is another high-priced, lazy veterinarian. John wants to be a farmer. Not some hot shot doctor!"

Kenji felt that Henry did not want to hear about anything but farming.

Kenji ran up the dusty stairs to the hayloft to load feed down into the chutes for the cows. He took a shiny shovel and began shovelling hay and the vitamin tablets into the chutes. The grain polished shovel gleamed like well-polished silver.

He soon finished shovelling the hay and the vitamin tablets into the chutes and descended down to join the others.

John was collecting milk in a bucket for a calf.

Fourteen

After breakfast, Kenji and George went down to the cool basement for a game of pool.

Kenji racked up the balls and George broke them.

"Keep it quiet down there!" Henry's voice called from upstairs.

"He's only upset with himself," said George. "No problem. The noise of the balls hitting each other reminds him of hailstones hitting the tractors."

"Yes," Kenji answered. "But how does one play pool quietly?"

"I don't know."

"I guess noise is part of the game."

"Like hailstorms a part of farming in Nebraska."

"Yes.'

"Will you be going out tonight to see Lisa, George?"

"No, I don't think so. She doesn't want to see me anymore."

"What happened?"

"Last night I jokingly said that she's still a little chubby for the coming summer beauty contest."

"George, you shouldn't say a thing like that, even as a joke."

"I know. It was a dumb thing to say. I apologized but she was too upset."

"I think she is very serious about that contest."

"She wants to compete in the State pageant if she wins."

"I hope she succeeds."

"Actually, it was my idea. I used to say 'if she ever got a body to match her pretty face, she'd win a beauty contest.' She used to be a chubby girl. And for the last two years she's been secretly dieting for the contest."

"That's hard to believe, since she is so slim."

"I know. She's a good-looking girl now.

Then they heard Henry calling them to go back to work. Both responded by returning up the stairs on the double.

After that conversation with George, Kenji had occasion to think of women in the most basic of comparative terms. George was very close and caring of Lisa, and usually able to relate with her on just about any level. The important issue that had escaped George was Lisa's vulnerability about her appearance. His age, of course, was the central factor in this lack of understanding.

And while most American men understood that such a vulnerability was common to many American women, despite their natural assets, Kenji could not help but find the situation baffling. And although he did not consider himself an expert on the Japanese female, he did have the innate instinctual feeling they enjoyed a lesser "sense of self" than did the American female.

Why? He had no idea. Again, a centuries-old sense of tradition likely played a role in the answer.

This was one of the many questions that plagued him for an answer, and which he might never live to understand.

Fifteen

Kenji stopped working momentarily to wipe the sweat from his brow. He wished he were swimming rather than working in the field on a hot day. Specifically, he wished he were swimming with Inga.

"Kenji, how's it going?" George asked, as he neared.

"Fine."

"Damned hot! I wish we could have a shower."

The two young men were now working side by side.

"Kenji, do you really love Inga?"

"Very much."

"Have you come to a decision yet?"

"No."

"So it's still eating away at your insides?"

"I feel terrible. How about you, George? Do you love Lisa?"

"Yeah."

"Are you going to marry her?"

"Certainly."

"Will you live in a city after you marry?"

"Yeah."

"Where?"

"Probably in G.I."

"So you are going to find a job there?"

"Yeah, as a mechanic."

"Good."

They quickly stopped talking when Henry neared them.

After they had set the irrigation, Henry took Kenji to the other side of the pasture on a tractor.

Stopping at the barbed-wire fence, Henry lifted the upper wire high up with his hand as he pushed the lower wire far down with his boot. Kenji bent his body carefully, entering the other side of pasture where there were much tall grass growing. And now Kenji held the wire for Henry as Henry had done for him.

In the grassy field, they bent their bodies hunting for the cantaloupes, hearing the sounds of grasshoppers at each of their steps. The field was full of crab-grass and foxtail-grass mixed together. Seeds of the grass stuck stubbornly to their trousers.

"They're just starting to get big. They'll be really big!" Henry said, happily, holding a matured cantaloupe in his hand. He took four melons with him when they left.

In the pasture, they picked the sticking grass seeds carefully off their trousers with their fingers and then loaded the cantaloupes on to the tractor. Kenji held two of them in his hands and the other two secured between his muddy boots on the floor of the muddy tractor.

Getting off from the tractor, each of them carried two cantaloupes into the house.

Kenji stamped his muddy boots against the ground to knock off the sun-dried mud.

Sixteen

A week passed and Kenji settled into the farm's routine. The work was hard, but now he knew what to expect, and what was expected of him. What he enjoyed most, perhaps, was that Henry was treating him less as a hired hand and more as a member of the family.

By now, Kenji knew a lot about Henry himself, about Henry's work, and about the unpredictability of Nebraska weather. In the back barn, Kenji leaned against the pitch fork and looked out to the empty corral through the opened sliding door. Not one of the cows could long stand in the hot sunlight; they were all in the cool shade of the trees.

"Kenji!" John's voice shouted out from the calf pen.

Kenji leaned the pitch fork against the wall and walked toward him. When he entered the calf pen, he was shocked at what he saw. A calf was dead!

The animal lay on the dirt floor, her four legs were stretched stiff and high in the air and she had an unnatural look. Her body was badly swollen, her rosy, thick tongue hung out and her eyes were opened wide. Flies buzzed about her.

"Poor calf. How come she died?" Kenji asked, wiping his forehead with the back of his hand.

"Because of this damn heat!" said John.

"Why is she so swollen?"

"She must have drunk a lot of water. They tend to do that when it's hot."

"What should we do?"

"I don't know, Kenji. Dad's gonna be furious when he finds out about this."

"Why don't you bring George here?" Kenji suggested.

"All right," he ran out of the barn.

Soon, John returned with George. George came in wiping his greasy hand with a cloth. He bent over and put his hand into the water bucket.

"John, this water is like hot soup!"

"I gave them cold water already," John protested.

"Bring some cold water quickly," said George, making a quick check of the other calves.

"Are they all right?" asked Kenji.

"They seem to be," George answered sharply.

John brought in cold water and they refreshed the calves with it.

"What should we do, George?" John asked, his eyes filling with tears.

"There's only one thing we can do. We'll take her right to the corn field. Dad won't know for a while. He'll think she disappeared on her own."

"I don't think it's a good idea to deceive your father like that," said Kenji, reproachfully.

"We have no choice," replied George.

"Kenji, help me carry her out," John asked, bending down to grab a hind leg.

"Me?" Kenji hesitated to touch the animal. "I can't. I just can't do it." Then, he looked at George, "Why don't you help John?"

"I can't. I have to watch for Dad."

Kenji reluctantly grabbed the other stiff leg. It was badly swollen and very cold.

They pulled the dead calf out together as the dust rose and the flies hovered. Kenji tried not to look at his burden as he pulled. Kenji suddenly felt an angry presence approaching.

Henry appeared out of nowhere. "What the hell are you two doing?" he screamed.

Then he looked down upon the dead calf's body.

"How could you be so careless, George?" he said, his face flushed red in rage.

"Don't blame this one on me. Blame the damn heat!" replied George.

"I already gave them cold water. But I'm sorry, Dad," said John.

Henry rubbed his forehead in thought. "Pull her to the yard! She ain't good for nothing now but dog food. I'll go in and make arrangements to have her picked up." Henry strode to the house.

Later that evening Kenji overheard Henry and Mary talking.

"Hank, why are you so tense tonight?"

"It's this damn farm. I try so hard. I try and I try and I try. But, damn it! It seems like its not worth it anymore. Why? Does God have something against me? If anything else happens I just may give up this farm."

"You're not serious, are you?"

"I'm giving it some serious thought, but I'm going to fight to the end. I'll fight to the last ear of corn." Then he turned his face upward and called to God: "You hear me? Give me your best shot. You'll never beat down Henry Harris!"

Seventeen

In the early afternoon of the next day, the warm wind began to blow steadily as Henry and George leaned over a piece of farm machinery; Henry had a wrench in his hand and George a spanner; their hands and faces were covered in oil and grease. John was caring for the calves while Kenji was feeding the pigs outside. A sudden gust shot dust into Kenji's eyes. He felt pain, and tears ran down his cheeks. Again the warm wind gusted, sending more dust into his face. Finally the wind took Kenji's cap away and he chased it.

"This is it! This is it!" Henry said to himself, looking up at the sky. High above the white cumulus the cirrus were feathers against the July sky. That sky was still blue and calm, and appeared unthreatening to Kenji. It was not even turning grey yet.

Then Henry quickly ordered the boys to move all the farm equipment to a safe place into the big garage or under the large trees.

Everyone moved quickly, like well-trained soldiers preparing for an upcoming enemy attack.

"Boss...! Boss...! Boss...!" Henry called to the head cow as the weather-vane, atop of the cupola of the barn, shook unsteadily as it pointed to the north. The TV antenna on the roof of the house shook violently and the trees and the corn stalks swayed. Several birds flapped away, caught in the current of the wind. Suddenly the head cow led all her sister cows in a line toward the corral.

Looking up at the sky, Kenji feared what a hailstorm would do to the corn. He hoped that no hail would fall on Henry's farm — but he wished, if possible, to see a hailstorm with his own eyes. He thought a good storm without hailstones might break up the monotony of farm life.

They all quickly put the tractors and cars into the large garage and under the trees.

The wind, a few minutes later, was beginning to soften and die down and everyone put all the equipment back into place.

Henry was breathing heavily; his eyes looked hollow and empty. There was a look of relief on his face like a man whose hanging had been postponed; it was a relief caused by postponement of the inevitable.

"That could have been it, Kenji," said Henry. "It could almost break a man's heart."

"It's strange that you stay on the farm when there's so much chance that everyday your entire crop could be totally wiped out. You're a skilled mechanic. You could earn really good money as a mechanic in town," said Kenji.

Henry looked at him with a mixture of contempt and pity. "You have to have been born on a farm to understand," he said slowly. "If you took me off the farm to a city, you could dig my grave in two months. When you can understand that you can really say you're a farmer."

"Today you're very lucky."

"On this same farm, my father, after he returned from the war, had only one hailstorm in his entire farming career. But I've already had three."

"It doesn't seem fair," said Kenji.

He looked up again at the clear blue Nebraska sky trying to understand meteorology.

Eighteen

"Now they're all here," Henry said proudly sitting on his muddy John Deere tractor in the pasture watching the cows.

The cows were carefully picking and thoughtfully chewing the grass much like a gourmet would roll a fine wine around in his mouth. To Kenji, they all looked like good thinkers. Several cows kept their eyes on Kenji meaninglessly while chewing their grass. Kenji remembered that one day all the cows tightly surrounded him when he was sitting in the pasture alone and studied him as if they had never seen a human being before. Probably, they had never seen an Oriental before, he thought.

"They're having a picnic on the grass," said Kenji to Henry sitting beside him.

"They sure are. They deserve it. They're all good cows."

While watching the cows, Kenji saw a car, across the barbed-wire, coming up on the dirt road blowing dust behind it. A girl was driving. He recognized her as Lisa, George's girlfriend. Kenji waved his hand and she waved back as she drove on. Then he looked over at Henry. Henry didn't even acknowledge her. He just looked in the opposite direction.

Kenji had to say something.

"Do you recognize which one is the head? The Boss?"

"I think it's that one," Henry pointed out a cow.

"She looks beautiful."

"You see, they all have different faces and marks just like we do."

"I see."

"Cows are like people, you know. Good ones and bad ones. Our cows all have good characteristics; polite, well-behaved, productive and cooperative.'

"Look at that grass! Very good grass. Very good pasture."

"Do they like this grass?" asked Kenji.

"Very much."

"Good."

"You know, all this land around here used to be pastures for grazing. But, as you see, not any more. All you can see is corn, corn and more corn," said Henry, very unhappily, gesturing across the horizon.

"Why?"

"Many of them switched to the corn business. Because today there are all kinds of good irrigation machinery. The good irrigation machinery changed some people's minds and farming habits. It's easier to raise good corn than it was before when we had to rely on only rainfall. That's why today we have too much corn in Nebraska."

"Too much?" Kenji asked thoughtfully. "Too much means the corn price goes down?"

"Damn right. It goes down...way down. Then farmers plant less corn...cut back on production. So what happen? There's less corn, and the price goes up again. Then the farmers plant more next year. And so on. It's a vicious cycle. But this year's gonna be great for us. I planted a lot and most everybody else didn't. And I've got better irrigation set up this year. Borrowed on my house to beef up my system so I should do really well this year. Of course, it doesn't mean a damn thing until you harvest it," he said, pausing and searching the sky for any indication of an approaching storm.

"Rabbit!" Kenji shouted with excitement. He spotted it

in a distance.

"Damn rabbit!" Henry yelled without excitement. "That's a jackrabbit."

The rabbit suddenly sat up and looked at Henry and Kenji distrustfully.

The rabbit took off as Kenji jumped off the tractor.

Kenji chased the rabbit but the rabbit easily avoided him zig-zagging between the legs of uninterested cows. As the rabbit tore through their territory, grasshoppers leaped out of the way making creaking sounds; some grasshoppers even bounced against the milk wells of the cows as they jumped up.

Kenji returned to the tractor, climbing up.

"I wish I had a shotgun with me."

"What's wrong with the rabbit?"

"Rabbits eat corn."

"I see."

"Kenji, look at that cow over there with all those black spots on her hide. Very unusual, don't you think?"

"I don't know. Why?"

"Look very carefully. The black spots have the shape of a young couple; man and woman are sitting tightly side by side and looking out. A good-looking couple."

"Oh, I see. I can see it now in the way you described it."

"And the couple is even casting their shadows behind them."

"Unique."

"Someday, I'm gonna hang that hide on my wall in my office." Henry seemed so serious.

"I don't like to think about that aspect of farm life," Kenji said sadly.

"She's very old, Kenji," replied Henry. "She has to retire soon. See her legs? They're not straight. Poor cow."

"What happens to her when she retires?"

"She pays a visit to the butcher for our food."

"You mean you kill her right away?"

"That's the law of the farm," said Henry. "You can't be sentimental."

Kenji could not argue with that so he decided to change the subject. "Which one is your favorite cow?"

"I love 'em all, Kenji," he replied. Then he started staring intently at one cow.

"What's wrong?" asked Kenji.

"Not a thing in the world," said Henry, breaking into a smile. "We're gonna have a baby calf. She's in labor now," he pointed out. Then he drove up a little closer to the cow.

On the tractor, Henry and Kenji watched the cow that was lying down, completely isolated from the others. She looked like she was in real pain. Suddenly, tiny front hooves appeared, followed by a wet small black and white head. Then came the slender black and white body and finally the back legs. For a few moments, the calf looked dead, then its legs jerked, and then jerked again. Finally, it tried to stand up with shaky rear legs providing little support. The calf tried again. And again. The mother stood quietly nearby, watching her new born, as if saying: "Try again! One more time! Just one more time!"

And then it made it! All four skinny little legs locked in place. The mother was cleaning the calf gently with her tongue and then led it toward the corral as if saying: "I will show you our home." The calf took one slow cautious step after another as the mother cow kept looking back at her new born baby while leading toward the corral where the shimmering large white barn stood against the blue sky.

They watched them until the mother and baby disappeared into the corral.

"That's what farming's all about, Kenji."

"Marvelous!" Kenji was amazed. Henry had probably seen it happen hundreds of times but he seemed deeply touched.

"I tell you what, Kenji. To commemorate the occasion of the calf's birth in honor of your work on the farm here, I'll name the calf Tokyo."

Kenji smiled in appreciation. "Thank you very much. Tokyo. Very nice. She will be a very good cow."

"After she gets pregnant and has a calf next year, she'll start to give milk. Until then, she gets everything for free."

"What if the calf had been a bull. What do you do with your young bull calves?"

"We feed them well, let them grow up, and after they're full grown, we sell them, to the market, for food." Henry made it all seem like a business proposition.

"Very sad," said Kenji, shaking his head and thankful that Tokyo was a female.

"That's the way it has to be. This is a dairy farm, not a cattle ranch. We raise cows for milking. Not steers."

"I understand but I can't accept it."

"John used to feel the same way when he was little. He had a favorite bull that I sold one day while he was at school. When he came home and found it gone, he cried for days. But he learned what life on the farm is all about. You have to understand that everything that happens on a farm is for a reason. And whatever happens is best for the farm."

Now Henry stopped the tractor and they both climbed off and walked through tall grass, grasshoppers leaping away at each their steps, showing off their colorful wings of gray, brown, yellow and vivid red. Kenji was hearing their loud creaks.

"Kenji, look here!" Henry said, pointing down.

There were several deep holes here and there.

"Who made those?"

"Badgers."

"What do they look like?"

"They're small animals with ugly-looking claws."

"Are their claws sharp?"

"Very sharp. They must have them so they can dig very well. That's how they survive, digging holes and eating anything small that gets trapped in the holes, even rabbits.

They're tough, too. When I was a young boy, my father put out a trap for one but the badger had chewed its back foot off to set itself free. The next day, my father set the trap again and this time we found a front paw."

"Incredible!"

All the while, they were walking through the pasture.

Henry stopped and asked. "Kenji, have you ever heard of the Oregon Trail?"

"Yes, I learned of it in American History."

"Well, these are the marks from the wagon wheels that came across the Oregon Trail." Henry pointed down to the two deep, hard-packed parallel ruts in the ground where no grass grew and which ran across the pasture then disappeared beyond the barbed wire fence of the pasture.

"Oh," said Kenji, looking down on it. "This is a very historical place!" he said with great curiosity, his eyes halting on the landmark momentarily. "That was a long time ago."

"Yes, a long time ago. In the 1850's at the height of the California Gold Rush. An estimated fifty thousand men, women and children passed along this trail in their covered-wagons, moving to the west. Hundreds of wagons used to come through here everyday on their way west. That's what my grandmother used to tell me when I was a young boy. So many wagons. So heavy with people and equipment — that's why these tracks are still here. Just as if set in concrete."

Kenji tried to visualize what it must have been like to have all those old wagons passing through here.

"Was this their only way west?"

"The only way."

"How long did it take?"

"Three months to get to California if they didn't die on the way from disease or snake bite or Indian attacks."

Momentarily, the Indian attacks were running in Kenji's mind as he had seen in the Western movies he remembered from his boyhood.

"Some call this the Oregon Trail or California Trail, because many of them went to Oregon or Washington for farming. Some of them went to California to look for gold and were called Forty-Niners."

Now Kenji and Henry got back on the tractor and started moving back to the house.

Henry was still overwhelmed by his beautiful cornfield so he did not see the two figures, George and Lisa, sitting on the lawn beneath a great maple tree by the house, but Kenji saw them.

When the couple saw the tractor approaching, they quickly slipped out of sight around the side of the house.

Henry was still looking at his corn. That was all that mattered to him.

That night, laying in bed and waiting for sleep to come, Kenji thought about Henry's obsession with corn, and with his ranch, and with his family. Kenji had never personally known a Japanese farmer or rancher or dairyman, but he wondered if the same kind of thinking would hold true halfway around the world and in a culture thousands of years older than this one. Regardless of the cultural dichotomy, the concerns of the family man on the Japanese farm would have to be the equivalent of Henry's concerns. The one would have to fret daily about bills and crops and animals and feed and family matters and so on, as would the other.

The output of the farming, or ranching, or dairying — that is, the eventual product — might be as diverse as rice and corn, milk and bread, trees and fish, but the central chores and demands of the lifestyle had to be roughly the same. In a word, the twin concepts of responsibility and obligation had to be the same despite the ten-thousand mile chasm separating the two worlds.

NINETEEN

Tokyo was now one day old. And Henry had said that she must be isolated from the other cows and put her in the calf pen. George, John and Kenji were the ones who would do it. Kenji was not looking forward to this at all. He thought it would be sad separating the young calf from its mother.

As Kenji accompanied the two boys to the corral where the cows were kept, he felt as though he were approaching a battle zone.

While the three mean bulls, all wearing nose rings, sat lazily around the edge of the corral, one hundred and nineteen cows stood up and made a wall between the three men who were approaching the new mother and Tokyo, who were sitting together by the water tank. They viewed the three visitors suspiciously, as if they were the enemy.

Now John left to get the pickup truck. Lucky John, Kenji thought.

"It seems it will be very difficult to move her away," said Kenji, as he approached the cows.

"I knew they would not give up the calf easily without a fight."

The calf's mother laid down next to her baby, making Kenji feel even worse. "I wonder if cows know anything about psychological warfare."

"Then we'd need machine guns to control them. Thank

118

God, they don't have any brain."

"It seems it's going to be a big fight."

"Kenji, be careful of the cows. If they're really mad, they'll kick you."

"George, I feel guilty for doing this...separating a day-old calf from its mother."

"You've been on a farm long enough to realize that emotions are not very important."

"I know."

"Kenji, you go to that side. I'll go over there."

They tried to separate the cows but it didn't work well.

The cows lowered their heads, mooing. Most of them lay down on the ground around the mother and the calf. Kenji felt both sad and useless. He was sad because he would have to separate a baby from its mother; he felt useless because he could not move any of the cows out of the way. Nor could John get the pickup truck near.

"We can't do anything now," said George.

"They're very upset."

"We better wait for Dad."

After they decided to wait for Henry to help them out, George and Kenji moved away from the cows, who were still on the ground, surrounding Tokyo and her mother. To Kenji, the cows looked like soldiers resting after a battle won. He was glad they had won.

"George, why don't we let Tokyo stay with her mother one more day? This seems very cruel."

"I know. But we have no choice. She has sucked many other cows' milk."

"Then, why not just separate her and her mother from the rest of the herd a few more days."

"That's a good idea."

Just then, Henry drove up on a big yellow tractor with a scooper attached to the front. George went over and told Kenji's suggestion to him.

"Get the hell over there and get that damn calf!" Henry

shouted from the tractor. "You act like you belong in a pen."

George and Kenji tried again. Again all the cows rose, except the mother cow and her baby calf who were still sitting together, but seemed a little less defiant. They seemed to know now that Henry was in charge and that this was not in their favor. The first thing Henry did was to put the tractor in gear and move back and forth busily and loudly in the muddy ground to scare the cows. The huge rear wheels of the tractor threw up large clumps of mud and finally the cows slowly retreated until only Tokyo and its mother were left. To Kenji, the tractor must have looked like a tank to the innocent cows.

Henry drove up close to the mother and calf, circled around them and the water tank several times to scare the mother, and then lowered the tractor's scooper so that its tips nearly grazed the cow's ears. Kenji felt that the mother was not much scared by the tractor. Finally, the mother stood up heavily and slowly walked away looking back at her baby.

George and Kenji reached over to the calf and grabbed her firmly but gently.

"Easy! Easy!" said Henry, lowering the scooper to the muddy ground next to the calf.

George and Kenji picked up the shuddering frightened calf and lifted her gently onto the scooper. On the scooper, George and Kenji grabbed her tightly but gently. Henry lifted all three of them and carefully drove the tractor and its precious cargo over to John who was waiting in the red pickup truck. Kenji looked into the calf's eyes and saw that she was gentle and innocent and very much afraid. She was also wet and muddy.

"Will she catch cold?" Kenji asked George.

"I don't think so."

Lifting the scooper ever so gently, Henry drove until it reached near the level of the bed of the pickup truck to unload the calf. Henry's delicate actions betrayed his rough orders. George and Kenji jumped off in the bed of the pick-up and carefully loaded her onto the bed. John started the engine when George hit the pickup with his hand saying: "Let's go!" Kenji stroked her gently as John drove off toward the barn.

On the bed, Kenji looked back. All of the cows were standing there motionlessly, staring at the pickup. He felt the cows knew they had been defeated but were still very angry.

Later on, as Henry and Kenji walked back to the house, Henry told Kenji, "There's a rodeo coming to Burwell. The whole family is going and we'd like you to come along. Would you be interested?"

"Yes, I have never seen a rodeo before."

Henry laughed and put his arm around Kenji's shoulder.

Twenty

As the days passed, Kenji's depression and emotional pain grew more intense, since he hadn't received any money from his family. He slowly realized that he had to stay on the farm for a longer period than he had expected and wait until he could make the money by himself to cover his travel expenses.

As the days passed, as the corn stalks grew high, George and Kenji became friendlier even though they had come from completely different backgrounds. So it was that George wanted to take Kenji to meet his grandparents who lived in Grand Island in the early evening after dinner.

They were driving along the country highway.

The first thing George naturally did was to turn on his radio allowing his hard rock to blast out loudly from the two back speakers. Kenji lowered the volume but George turned it back up.

"George, slow down!"

"Don't worry. I've never had an accident."

"You're only nineteen. You haven't been driving long enough."

"Driving since ten is long enough. I feel like I'm a hundred years old when it's all been spent on a farm." George then pushed the pedal down a little further.

"You'll get a ticket."

"I don't care."

"George, do other farm boys also start to drive that early?"

"Sure. What else is there to do in spread-out land like ours?"

"I guess you're right."

"Kenji, my grandfather drinks a lot once in a while. I don't want you to feel bad, if he says some thoughtless things about Japanese. Because when he was a soldier he fought against Japanese troops during World War Two."

"Oh, no problem."

It did not take very long by the way George drove. They were soon in Grand Island. The town looked deserted; all the shops were closed and no one was walking on the sidewalks. A little dog, scampering down the side of the street, was the only pedestrian in sight.

Off in the distance, Kenji saw a train. George saw it too.

"I want to show you something," George said to Kenji.

The car began to pick up speed and began hurtling down a two lane street.

"Is your seat-belt on?" George asked.

"Yes."

Kenji noticed the blinking railroad crossing ahead.

"What are you doing?" Kenji asked nervously.

"Just watch."

The train was getting closer and the bells were becoming louder. Kenji wanted to close his eyes but his sight was riveted to the approaching crossing and train.

It looked like George was about to smash into the train ahead. George simultaneously turned the steering wheel while yanking the emergency brake hard. The back of the car skidded, turning the car completely around in the opposite direction, he then hit the gas and they began speeding off again away from the train.

"George, what's wrong with you?" Kenji loudly

demanded.

"I just wanted you to see what a great driver I am."

"You're not a great driver! You're a dangerous driver!"

"You're too serious, Kenji."

Kenji didn't want to speak to George. He was very upset.

On the other side of town, they slowly drove through a residential area.

Now George pulled off onto a narrow, country dirt road. They passed many cottonwood trees and shrubs before Kenji finally saw a small, old white trailer on the right-hand side in the distance near a small lake and there were many cottonwood trees and shrubs around the lake.

"That's my grandparents' home!" said George with some excitement.

George parked in front of the trailer. Kenji saw two fishing poles pitched into the soft sand against the dark reflection of cottonwood trees and shrubs in the calm water. It was a very peaceful and relaxing scene.

"Robert, they're here now!" came an excited voice from inside the trailer.

George and Kenji got out of the car as an older woman, with short gray curly hair, stuck her head out the door and smiled.

"Grandma, this is Kenji."

"Hello, Kenji," she said, coming out of the trailer. She was a very heavy woman.

"Hi," said Kenji.

"I'm very glad to meet you," she put out her hand. "My name is Carol."

"Nice to meet you, Carol." Kenji liked her warm, firm hand shake. Her arms seemed heavy.

"You have a pretty good tan, Kenji," she said. "First thing that happens to a farmer."

"He's a real dumb farmer now," added George jokingly.

Carol smiled.

When they were all in the trailer Kenji looked around inside. Orange seemed to be the main theme; everything was either partially or completely orange. Bright orange curtains dropped down from along orange velvet draperies which touched the deep orange carpets and provided the background for the black and orange checked sofa. Above the sofa, there were many framed colored photos of Henry, Mike, John, George and Mary and the rest of the family. Bright and clean, the trailer had a place for everything. And everything was in its proper place. It was a very small and cozy home and reminded Kenji quite a bit of the small houses that many Japanese live in.

An older man, who had white short hair, wearing gray trousers and white sleeveless shirt, walked up from one end of the trailer and George introduced him to Kenji. He was a large man like his son Henry.

"Hello, Kenji. I'm Robert." They shook hands.

"I recognize you from your pictures," Kenji said. He felt the many callouses on the man's hand. A farmer's hand, he thought.

"Very glad you're here. We've heard a lot about you. How's it going with your car?"

"Oh, they finally got the parts and they're fixing it."

"Good. Hope it won't be any problem."

Robert, George and Kenji sat down on the comfortable sofa.

"I'll make some coffee," Carol said happily.

"How was your fishing trip, Grandpa?"

"It was O.K. But we couldn't catch any fish. Only a few small bass. And in one place we had a shower so the hilly dirt road turned to sticky clay so we couldn't get out of the place so we had to stay overnight until the sun came out and dried the muddy road.'

"And, you know, there aren't many fish in the rivers these days because the farmers are using so much water to irrigate the fields. It's causing the rivers to go dry," Robert said bitterly.

The aroma of freshly-brewed coffee quickly filled the small trailer as she carried a plate of cookies. "I hope you like chocolate chip cookies. I baked them today."

Kenji tasted one. "Delicious."

"Good. I'm glad you like it," she said.

"George," said Robert, "have you heard from Mike recently?"

"Yeah, we received a letter from him two weeks ago. He's doing all right. And he plans to come home this fall to go hunting."

"Sounds good. I wonder if he's going to re-enlist?"

"I don't know. He didn't mention anything about it."

"The Navy's good for him. See the world. Learn new things."

That doesn't sound like a farmer talking, thought Kenji as she poured the coffee.

"Grandpa was a Marine," George said to Kenji. Then leaning to his grandfather, "I don't think Dad would be too happy to hear you talk like that."

"Oh, Henry's got farming on his brain all the time. It's too much, too much," Robert said to George. Then he turned to Kenji. "I was a farmer for forty-five years. Look what I've got to show for it." He held up his hands in front of Kenji. His fingers were badly misshaped and curved.

"You must have worked very hard," Kenji stretched out his hand and gently touched the hardened curved hand.

"That's what forty-five years of gripping a tractor wheel everyday will do to you." He said it matter-of-factly without any bitterness.

"Do you still farm?" Kenji asked.

Robert laughed a little. "Naw. Those days of mine are gone forever. Thank goodness. They say farmers retire only when they die. I guess I'm the exception. I've had enough of that. Time to have a good time now. Let someone else have all the worry and headaches. Let Henry have it all. He enjoys it. He believes the world begins and ends with farming."

Kenji could now understand why George liked to come here and visit his grandparents. Robert was everything that Henry wasn't.

"If you had to do it all over again, would you choose farming as a career again?" asked Kenji.

"Nope. Not one chance in a million."

Carol added. "We don't believe in all this newfangled irrigated land. If God would only give us rain, it would be just fine; if not, that would also be fine."

"Mostly all we enjoy now is fishing. We fish the whole summer, here and there, in Nebraska. And in October, we pull this trailer on down to Texas and fish there until the spring. In spring we come home here again," said Robert.

"You don't miss farming even a little bit?" Kenji asked.

"I never even think about it except to wonder why I did it for so long. Forty-five years. Can you believe that?"

"I thought you said fifty-five years before," said Kenji a little shyly.

"Forty-five. Fifty-five. Hell, it seemed like a hundred."

Kenji looked over at George, who was laughing. So that was where George had got some of his best lines, Kenji thought.

Robert continued. "Sold the farm, invested a little, killed off a little time, and then we bought this trailer with the rest. Haven't looked back since."

Kenji noticed that Carol had not said that much. Like Japanese women, Kenji thought. In fact, she seemed to be a great deal like her daughter-in-law, Mary. Maybe farm women are all reserved, thought Kenji.

Finally, she spoke up. "That's right. This trailer and pickup truck are our whole world since we sold the farm." She seemed as happy about that decision as her husband.

"So, George, how's everything on the farm?" asked Robert. He did not sound as though he really cared but was just making polite conversation.

"Oh, the usual, you know."

Robert nodded his head, smiling in agreement. Obviously, George and Robert shared similar attitudes about Henry and his devotion to farming. Kenji was surprised that Henry voluntarily let George come out and see this man. It would seem that Robert would be a very bad influence on George.

The conversation went on with most of the talk being about anything but farming. George's grandparents were asking about his friends, male and female, his car, his plans. Kenji was surprised that George did not talk much about Lisa, about the upcoming beauty contest, but his grandparents wished she would win the beauty contest which would be held tomorrow night. They did not treat him like the thankless inheritor of the Harris farm that Henry was making him out to be. They treated him as a young man, not a young farmer. Kenji liked that and so did George.

The night ended much too early for Kenji and George but Robert and Carol were old and so they tired easily at night. Kenji had a wonderful time which he said so over and over again as they said goodbye to the old couple.

George and Kenji got into the car and George revved up his engine and they took off.

Twenty-One

"What a difference between your father and your grandfather! Like the difference between you and your father."

"I really like Grandpa. I wish my Dad were more like him," said George as he drove. "He has a more realistic view of things."

"Well, I guess your father has a lot of pressure these days. Lots of responsibilities."

"I know that farmers are having a hard time today, but he's too intense. I don't mean he should sit around doing nothing."

"I think your father reminds me my father. My father keeps working without taking any vacations."

"You know what I think? I think my Dad is living out his military fantasies with the farm like he's a general and our family is his army and the farm is the nation he's been sworn to protect."

"I think you're exaggerating."

"I'm not."

"Was your father also a Marine?"

"No. He was never in the service. His father was in it, and now his oldest son is, but he never was. He married young so he didn't have to go."

"I see."

"Hey, Kenji, you wanna stop for a beer?"

"All right. But how can you drive back home after drinking?"

"No sweat! I've been doing it for years," George replied.

"A hundred years?" teased Kenji.

"Yup."

George pulled the car into a sleazy-looking bar where the half neon sign of a white champagne glass with bubbles, blinking on top of the roof, did not work. In the parking lot were parked many old cars.

Outside it was quiet, but when George opened the door, the bar exploded with smoke and noise and light. About twenty people were dancing to country music from the jukebox and a dozen were leaning against the bar clapping to the music and drinking beer. George and Kenji sat at a small table.

George ordered beers. The bartender brought the two bottles of beer and two glasses. George paid him and gave him a tip. Both of them made a toast to Lisa to win the beauty contest tomorrow. They drank silently and watched the dancers.

"You know, Kenji, actually, I'm afraid of Lisa winning the beauty contest tomorrow."

"Why?"

"If she wins I'll lose her forever."

"I understand what you mean, George. But you shouldn't feel that way."

"I know. Of course, I hope she'll win tomorrow."

When the music ended, all the dancers scattered to their tables and the counter to drink their beers.

George stood up and went to the jukebox to put in a couple of quarters. But he came back to the table with his quarters still in his hand.

"Nothing on that box but redneck music."

"What's redneck music?" Kenji asked.

"Like the stuff my Dad plays all day."

"Stuff?"

"Country music."

"Oh."

"My father would like this place."

One of the three bearded men at the next table, overhearing the conversation, stood up and asked George, "You got somethin' again' country music, boy?"

George looked at them nervously, "It's O.K. if you're a boring old fool."

"You callin' me a borin' old fool, boy?" demanded the bearded man.

"Nope," said George non-chalantly. "We were just joking."

"You think we ain't got no sense-a-humor?"

George did not reply.

The other two bearded men joined their friend standing around the table. Kenji feared that George had an excellent chance of getting his head ripped off in the next couple of minutes. But George was in a good mood. Probably the visit to his grandparents had cheered him up a great deal, Kenji thought. And his talking about Lisa had relieved his mind about that, too. He looked confident and radiated a certain strong self-possession about himself. George looked at the bearded men but did not say anything. There was a silent moment for a few seconds. A few seconds too long for Kenji.

"I was just upset because I couldn't find any of my type of music." said George.

The bearded men mumbled to themselves and sat back at their table.

George and Kenji breathed a deep sigh of relief.

George and Kenji drank their cold beers in silence and when they finished their beer, stood up, said good-bye to the older men and exited the door.

When they were safely inside their car, George suddenly started laughing hysterically. He could not stop and it was highly infectious. Kenji joined in the laughter. While still laughing, George suddenly mimicked the bearded men. "You callin' me a borin' old fool, boy?" He said in an exaggerated drawl.

For reasons he did not fully understand, Kenji found himself enjoying the situation every bit as much as George.

Twenty-Two

After Sunday dinner, George and Kenji went to town to see the summer beauty contest. They were both excited as they pulled into the parking lot, which was already jammed with many cars.

Kenji knew that George and Lisa hadn't seen each other for a few days and that she had not even invited George to the important event.

They walked into the pavilion where the contest was being held. Brightly colored flags decorated everything and the crowd seemed to be in very high spirits. Everyone seemed to wearing their best apparel as did George and Kenji with their blue jeans. The seats were jammed with people. A high-school marching band in colorful uniforms sat next to the stage playing up-beat music, apparently warming up everyone, for what was about to come. It was fast becoming clear to Kenji that Nebraska was America. Utterly typical America.

"I can't wait to see Lisa in a bathing suit," said George impatiently.

"She must be a knock-out dressed that way."

Then the band switched to soft music and all the girls came out on the stage, greeted by eager applause. Thus the beauty contest began.

"Boy, she looks great, doesn't she, Kenji?"

"Absolutely."

George did not readily identify Lisa when she was introduced, as being his Lisa.

"She looks like a different girl."

"She is beautiful."

"She is very slim, isn't she?" said George.

"Yeah. I think she's going to win."

"She stands a pretty good chance."

"She will make it."

Lisa told the crowd a little about herself, and then, as part of the talent portion of the contest, she did a beautiful tap dance to the tune of "Yankee Doodle Dandy," honoring America.

The performance was very polished and earned her thunderous applause.

"What a talent she has!"

"She's definitely going to win," George said with pride. He paused for a moment, then added, "Kenji, I really love her."

"It's good to love. Very good," replied Kenji. Suddenly he thought about Inga, wishing she were here. But he didn't want to say anything to detract from George and Lisa's night.

The swim suit competition began and Lisa looked wonderful.

"She has nice long legs," said Kenji.

"Definitely."

George was cheering loudly as if he were trying to influence the judges. George and Kenji compared all the girls to Lisa, one by one, as they were introduced and paraded in front of the judges.

Kenji was happy to see that George was so involved. Since Kenji had arrived at the farm, he mostly had seen George as a negative person. George didn't like farming, his Dad's attitude, and being stuck on a farm. It felt good to see George feeling so positive about something.

They looked up to the stage as a man in a business suit approached the microphone. "And the winner is... Lisa Snyder!"

"She did it, Kenji!" George began jumping up and down cheering at the top of his voice. "She did it!"

"This must be a perfect night for Lisa," said Kenji.

George sat back down and turned to Kenji and said, "She finally got what she wanted, what she worked for."

"Surely."

"C'mon Kenji, we gotta go down and congratulate her!" Without waiting for an answer he grabbed Kenji's arm and pushed his way through the crowd down to the stage where the new queen and the other contestants were posing for pictures.

She was busy greeting people. Her face lit up even more when she saw George and Kenji. Tears began rolling down her cheeks. George seemed to want to grab her but instead just stood there talking to her as if she were only an old family friend.

"Well, were you scared?"

"Oh yes, I was terrified."

"Are you happy?"

"I'm ecstatic! Aren't these flowers lovely?"

"I'm really happy for you," said George.

"Thank you so much," she said in the same voice she would use when talking to a favorite uncle.

"Can we go somewhere and talk, Lisa."

"Well, I have to stay here and have my picture taken."

"Can we talk after that?"

"Well, there's a dance after the pictures and I'm supposed to be there."

Without replying, George turned and left. Kenji followed behind.

George got into the car and opened the passenger side

for Kenji. George didn't even turn on the rock music the way he always did. Instead he and Kenji silently drove down the dark road.

Twenty-Three

The ride back the beauty contest was long and quiet. Kenji could understand why George was so depressed, and felt sorry for him.

"Let's just go back home and sit up in the barn for a while. That's a good place to talk."

"All right," Kenji answered.

They crept the car up to the house, so that no one inside would overhear, and parked quietly alongside the barn. They slipped out of the car quietly and carefully opened the barn door. If anyone was to see them, they would think they were burglars. Once into the dark barn, they climbed upstairs into the loft. George turned on a small light bulb so they could see and the two of them lay back comfortably against the hay.

"You know, Kenji, I really blew it. I was gonna start some racing with my Chevy, move out of here, marry Lisa and get a job in Grand Island as a mechanic. I had it all set up perfectly with Lisa. But now I don't know what I should to do," he added in a low depressed voice.

"Well, George, you still have all of that, except for Lisa."

"I know. But, I needed her to make this all work. That's why I wanted to do all of that stuff."

Kenji realized that if he hadn't loved Inga he probably

wouldn't have attempted to across the country in a car. Somehow I had a self-actualized spirit at that time, he thought to himself.

"George," Kenji said suddenly, "why don't you try all of that without her."

"It wouldn't be the same. I wouldn't be doing it for the right reasons."

"She might change her mind, George." Kenji felt this sounded as if he was talking to himself about his father.

"I don't think so."

"She didn't say she never wanted to see you again, did she?"

"Well, no. Not exactly."

"Maybe you have a wrong feeling. Maybe things will change in a few weeks or a few months. Right now she's too excited about winning the contest. She has too many things on her mind. Give her some time."

"I can't wait!" George said with frustration. "I want something to happen now!"

"You're impatient, George. Take it easy."

"I guess I should just bide my time."

"Sometimes you have to wait for things to work themselves out. They will, if they're supposed to."

"I guess you're right. But, I want her right now! I can't wait!"

There were a few moments of awkward silence. The silence was broken by the shuffling noise coming from the young cows downstairs. Kenji did not pay much attention, but George immediately sat up and said:

"Something's wrong!"

"What?"

"I've lived on a farm too long not to realize what it means when the animals get uneasy."

"Maybe somebody's messing around with the cows.

"Maybe they sense something we don't."

"I wish they could talk," said Kenji.

"Yes, I wish they could talk, too."

George sniffed the air a couple time then reacted.

"My God! Smoke! There's a fire!"

"Where, George? Where?"

"I don't know where," he said, frantically, "but it's around here! If we don't find it and put it out right now, we're in big trouble! This place'll go up in about thirty seconds!"

They quickly moved around the loft trying to find the smoke. The loft was dark and this made their job even more difficult. They were across the barn from each other. In the loft, Kenji finally saw smoke in a corner about fifteen feet from him. He quickly picked up a small flour sack and tried to beat out the smoke and smoldering fire. Suddenly, a small fire erupted right in front of him, almost burning his face as the flames leapt up, attacking him.

"Fire! Fire! Over here! Over here!"

George came running over from the other side of the barn and by now the flames were reaching to the roof and the smoke was intense, almost blinding. Kenji was stunned by the sudden intensity of the fire, slightly overcome by the smoke, so that he was laying back on some hay trying to get his breath.

"Kenji! Kenji! Are you all right?"

He nodded to George that he was all right, but the smoke was becoming so heavy it almost blanketed the corner of the loft. Kenji was not feeling as well as he was a few minutes before. He had inhaled too much smoke and had begun to cough uncontrollably.

The smoke was now affecting George too. He took off his cap and covered his mouth as best as he could. But once safely away from the fire and smoke, both men were able to breath normally again.

"Let's get all the young cows out! Hurry!" shouted George, jumping down the stairs. Kenji followed him.

While George opened the sliding door, Kenji ran to the

pen to let all the young cows out. At this time he knew he did not have to open the gate of the pen. All the calves were prostrate in the pen. They looked as though they were asleep, but, in truth, their lungs were filled with smoke. They had suffocated.

Abandoning everything, Kenji and George ran out toward the house screaming: "Fire! Fire!"

From the house, Henry came running outside with a look of disbelief on his face. "Where's the fire?"

"The loft, Dad. The loft!"

Henry looked toward the top corner of the barn where the fire was concentrated. "Don't just stand there! Get the calves out of the barn!"

"Too late, Dad."

As the dense smoke began to escape from the opened sliding door and the cracks in the siding, Henry immediately turned and ran back into the house and took the telephone, angrily calling the fire department.

"Kenji!" screamed George, "get a hose and start watering down the milk house!"

George and Kenji started to run back to the barn to do whatever they could to contain the fire until help arrived, but the fire was already out of control.

Flames were coming out through the roof and sides of the barn, smoke billowing into the night, cows ominously mooing in the corral, worrying about their baby calves that had already died in the barn. The smell of burned animal flesh came out from the burning barn, and now the fire department, sirens wailing in the distance, were coming closer. Kenji was trying to spray water on a fire that could not be contained. It was incredible how fast the barn had erupted in flame and was being destroyed.

The fire trucks pulled into the farmyard but the fire-fighters never had a chance. It seemed that everything was out of control within ten minutes of the fire starting. You could not really fight that kind of fire. All you could do was to get out of its way.

And then it was over. The barn, so peaceful, so productive, had been devastated. There was no feature of a barn left to see. Only the silo stood alone. But the producing cows were all saved because they were in the corral. But all the calves, including Tokyo, lying in their pen, were unable to flee.

In the dark night, Henry was standing alone. Everyone tried to comfort him but he waved them all away. He just stood there, surveying what only an hour before had been the pride of his life. Now it had all been reduced to a few blackened timbers standing against the darkness. The milking equipment was rendered useless. Henry stood there for a very long time and stared. Like a stubborn bull, he would not move. He did not even seem to breath. Suddenly, he turned and walked into the house. Kenji and George were standing in the kitchen. Henry stormed into the kitchen.

"What were you doing in the barn?" he angrily demanded of George.

"Me and Kenji..."

"I'm not talking about Kenji. I'm talking about you, boy!"

"Well, we got home and we..."

"I didn't even hear you come home."

"We sort of came home quietly to the barn and climbed up into the loft and sat there and talked," he answered lamely.

Kenji wanted to say something, but Henry was no longer treating him as one of the family.

"What the hell were you doing in the loft? Drinking?"

"What are you talking? I told you Kenji and me were up there and..."

"Leave Kenji out of this, I said!"

"O.K....I was up there and I turned on the light and..."

"You what!" Henry looked as if he was going to explode.

"I said I turned on the light."

"You know that bulb had a bad connection! I was just telling your mother tonight that we have to fix that wiring problem up there."

"Hey, I've been gone all night. How would I know that?" George asked, almost in tears.

"Don't give me any of your smart-mouth. You should have known the wiring up there was bad."

"How?"

"It's been bad for years," Henry replied.

"Then why didn't you fix it? If you had any insurance, we could build a new barn." George started to walk away from Henry.

"Don't throw the blame on me, boy. That's your whole problem. You always blame someone else for your foul-ups."

"Have a nice life," George told Henry as he turned to face him. Then as he walked upstairs, he added, "I'm taking off."

Mary started to go after him but Henry's look restrained her. It was almost as if Henry wanted George to leave.

Out the kitchen window, Kenji could see the last of the fire trucks pulling away and the battered remnants of the barn reflecting in the moonlight. Kenji felt sad, thinking how the barn was gone and how all the calves were dead. Everyone, except George, sat around the kitchen table. Very little was said.

While Henry made several calls to some neighbors for help in taking care of the cows he had left, Kenji heard foot-steps bounding down the stairs and then outside he heard a car door slam. Hearing the engine sound, Kenji ran out of the kitchen. The last thing he saw was George's Chevy rapidly disappearing down the dirt road.

Is he leaving the farm? If so where is he going? Hope he comes back, Kenji said to himself. He felt bad for the Harris family. And in an odd way, he felt somewhat responsible for the fire. Maybe George would not have gone up into the loft if he had not been with him or perhaps he should have talked George out of it. He felt even worse thinking about the cows that would have to be taken away somewhere else.

Later that night many neighboring dairy farmers came with their livestock vans and started to load all the cows to take them away. It was a long night.

It seemed very strange to Kenji to be a first-hand observer to an American tragedy — indeed, almost a participant. This was the kind of tragedy that happened the world over, except that in certain parts of the world — notably Japan — family tragedy was kept very private and seemingly unemotional. While here in America, everyone in the bereaved or otherwise injured family thought nothing of making a public display of their feelings, the Japanese family would cloak the whole event in near — ceremonial stoicism.

Twenty-Four

A postcard arrived three days later. It was from Texas. From George. He was staying in an apartment with a man he had met. He did not say anything about missing his family or friends or how much he cared about them.

Henry had not forgiven him or the way he had left. But he did miss him, both as a helper and as a son. He said that George would one day get all the wanderlust out of his system and come back home and be ready to settle down. Mary, of course, was very upset. She asked, what was so terrible about staying home? Couldn't he have just gone into Omaha? Why did he have to go so far away? What if he gets hurt? Or what if he doesn't have enough to eat? Listening to Mary, Kenji felt he was listening to his own mother. She had said the same things to him. Indeed, he missed George as much as anyone. They had had good times together. Kenji hoped he would change his mind and come back. Kenji still felt somewhat responsible for the fire, and still felt guilty that George might not have left the farm if Kenji had not been on the farm. John seemed to have matured greatly since George left. He probably had the best handle on the situation of anyone in the house. Also, he suggested that George would have left anyway and that this event just sped things up. After everyone read the postcard, Mary placed it on one of the pages of the photo album.

Saturday morning, after breakfast, Henry decided to take his family, including Kenji, to a Nebraska rodeo.

"We still have our chores to do and our lives to live. We can't stop everything just because something negative happened. We've got to keep going. It may turn out better for everyone. Last night I was thinking that I might do just as well raising milk cows and selling them to someone else and let other people do the milking. Just raise the cows, no longer a dairy! In any case, we can't do anything about it right now. Life goes on and so should we," said Henry.

No one could really argue with that logic. But the face and character of the Harris farm had changed so completely over the last three days with no barn and no George that it was hard for anyone to figure out what would happen next. The one thing that Henry was determined to do was to avoid dwelling on what had happened and what could not be changed.

John volunteered to stay on the farm to take care of it. So, Henry, Kenji and Mary set out to go to the rodeo. In some ways, it was the highlight of Kenji's summer, and to Henry it seemed like the perfect thing to get his mind off what had happened to his farm lately.

Henry naturally played country music while he was driving on the highway. He was the same as he had always been, passing out opinions and making judgments. He offered a running commentary to Kenji on the passing countryside, talking about how beautiful the cottonwood trees are, because they do not require much water; how bad sunflowers are, since they need large amounts of water; and how some rivers run dry because farmers remove too much water to irrigate their crops, yet seem to be without guilt. The highway smelled sweet from corn and newly-mown alfalfa.

"Look there, Kenji!" Henry said. He pointed out to an empty field on their right-hand side as they drove by. "That's the kind of damage a hailstorm does. The crops had been leveled, with not a single stock of corn remaining," Henry spoke in a solemn tone of voice as if giving the eulogy at a funeral.

Kenji was shocked. It was worse than he could ever had imagined. "When did that happen?"

"Probably a week ago."

"I didn't hear anything about it on the news," said Kenji.

"They happen often enough that it's not big news...unless it happens to your field."

"It makes me sick when I see all that destruction," Mary sighed. "It could have been us."

After seeing the havoc of the corn field, the three of them were quiet for the next few minutes until Henry turned off the highway and onto a narrow, loosely-graveled road.

Leaving a faint cloud of dust behind the car and the sound of gravel, which rubbed together and rebounded against the underside of the car-carriage as they drove upward toward the top of the hill where Henry's aunt, Tease, and uncle, Roy, lived.

At the foothill, Henry pointed out as he was driving and said to Kenji, "Mike killed a deer right there last year."

"Are there many deer around here?"

"Yep."

Reaching the uppermost part of the hillside, you could see a cornfield that spread out peacefully but the corn stalks were very short because it was nonirrigated land. The cornstalks standing along the roadside were covered with dust.

"Terribly dry corn! Sad corn!" Henry said.

They drove continuously toward the top of the hill, steadily climbing up the sharp angled dirt road.

Finally, after a sharp curve, was seen an old large cedar colored barn on the left side and a sun-faded blue two-story wooden house further up the peaceful hill on the right. About the house were many fine trees. At the far corner of the yard, a piece of two-by-four extended in the air to make an upper track for the garage's sliding door. A two-by-four brace was toenailed into the supporting beam. In between, the high grass leaned toward the unseen slope and the garage reflected the rosy pink of the sun. In front a knee-high water pipe paralleled the sun-baked concrete path. Two old wooden wagon wheels, also cedar colored, were leaning side by side in the flower bed for decoration. Broad cottonwood trees surrounded the barn and many cicadas were making summer sounds. On the other side was a machinery shed.

As Henry pulled the station wagon up into a dirt parking space in front of the house, the elderly couple, Henry's aunt and uncle came out, smiling.

Henry introduced Kenji to them and they welcomed him heartily. When Kenji shook the old man's big hand he could feel his hard calloused skin wrapped with warm feelings.

"You have such beautiful hills," said Kenji to Roy.

"Thanks," said Roy.

"We're now on the highest mountaintop in Nebraska, Kenji," said Henry, jokingly.

"I thought there weren't even any hills in Nebraska." Kenji smiled.

While Mary went into the house with Tease, Roy wanted to show Kenji the hills on his old jeep. All three men climbed up into the vehicle. Kenji sat beside Roy and Henry sat in the back seat. Roy was driving slowly, up and down, along the ruts, on the top of the hill, where the grass had been worn out by the tires. The two lines looked as hard as the Oregon Trail in Henry's pasture. The hills were covered with dry grass and dotted with a few bushes in the ravines.

Roy was explaining to Kenji happily, as he drove, about how he was the owner of the vast hills and he has been renting the other side of lower hills to other farmers for their cornfields. A cool breeze on the hills made the grass wave gently. A sandy brown rabbit was running away across the hill. "That's a cottontail!" shouted Henry, as it disappeared into a ravine. On the other side of the hill stood several cows gathered by a small pond.

In the distance, an airplane was flying across the hill. It looked very small from here; it shone brightly in the sun and the engine made vibrations that carried into the peaceful hills.

Now they returned to the house for a buffet lunch. Inside it was nice and cool.

In the dinning room, they all sat at the table covered with a soft red tablecloth and enjoyed roast turkey with gravy, various fresh salads, newly baked bread and chocolate cake served in bowls and crystal dishes. Red wine was served in luxurious wine glasses.

The house itself did not remind Kenji of George's grandparents, but the people did. Uncle Roy was also a retired farmer and his fingers were also badly curved inside like Henry's father, Robert. "From years of holding a tractor steering wheel, as well," Roy said. Tease was not so terribly different from Henry's mother, Carol. They were both quiet, letting their men do most of the talking, confining themselves to fixing meals and cleaning up afterwards. Kenji felt these women had to be more assertive in private but when with visitors they simply deferred to their husbands.

After their wonderful lunch, Roy and Tease joined them on their trip to the rodeo. The car was full of laughter and conversation. Kenji was glad to see Henry and Mary laughing so much because these days farming did not provide many laughs. This was not the original trip that Henry planned since Kenji came into his life, and now this invitation seemed somewhat empty of the generosity he had first extended to his hired hand.

Half an hour later, they all became extremely excited as they passed a large banner that stretched across the highway that said: WELCOME TO BURWELL, HOME OF NEBRASKA'S BIGGEST RODEO!

Henry pulled off into a dirt parking lot that was full of pickup trucks and recreational vehicles. They parked their car and started to walk among the huge crowd of people, mostly farmers and their families, that had congregated around the large display of farm tools and equipment.

"Farmers looking at new equipment," said Henry to Kenji, "is like women looking at new dresses. Every once in a while they buy one, but mostly they just look."

"Window-shopping," Kenji smiled.

On the way to the ticket windows, the five of them slowed their pace, examining and comparing manufacturers' competing models of machinery. Henry happily showed Kenji all the improved machinery for irrigation.

While Henry was engrossed with machinery, Kenji focused on an attractive, brunette teenager in cowgirl attire. She was leading a well-groomed brown horse with white stockings that sported a highly polished saddle trimmed in silver. The girl and the horse strutted proudly through the display grounds. They should be in a movie, Kenji said to himself.

They passed through the farm equipment show and walked toward the rodeo area. Some cowboys on crutches, who had either injured or broken their legs, were mixing with the crowd.

Henry bought five tickets, one for each of them, and they made their way through the crowd toward the middle of the grandstand shaded by a corrugated tin roof. The posts supporting it were old waiting to collapse under their own weight. But compensating for that drabness were the festive colors of the crowd and the arena's decorations. Every upright was adorned with bright flags and pennants.

They sat and, even though underneath the shade, they did not take off their caps because it was a very hot afternoon, and everyone — particularly those seated in the hot sun — wore colorful caps or hats and energetically fanned themselves with their programs. Far off, across the empty smooth reddish-brown dirt arena, on their left-hand side, were several contestants leaning against the wooden chute fences talking to one another. Kenji could feel the excite-

ment growing as more than three thousand people sat waiting — the joyful roar of their voices sounded like ocean
waves smashing against rocks.

With a sudden, joyful burst of applause from the audience, the loudspeakers blared forth: "Ladies and
Gentlemen...the rodeo will now begin!" A cowgirl on a stun-
ning white horse paraded into the arena, carrying a big,
bright American flag that flapped energetically in the warm
summer air. She was accompanied by another rider who carried a brightly-colored red rodeo flag. Following them were
many other boys and girls carrying flags on their horses. The
red, white and blue of the flags played off brilliantly in the
sun against the arena floor. High school bands in their colorful, shiny uniforms marched briskly, playing their music
joyfully. A large, middle-aged woman in tattered clothes
tugged at a playful, balky pony. The pony was dressed in
patched overalls and a small, slanted straw hat. Everyone
laughed heartily at the clowning pair. Then several covered
and topless wagons, filled with many small children, all
smiling and waving eagerly to the crowd, and pulled by big
and heavy-footed horses, rolled by. In the arena, everyone in
the parade lined up ceremoniously and filed out in a single
line to the enthusiastic applause of the crowd.

Finally, the main events began — the riding, the roping,
the tying, the wild-west confrontation of man and beast.

"Do you think the rodeo is a sport?" Kenji asked Henry.

"Damn right! Rodeo is America's number one sport!"

Kenji was not sure it was a sport, making animals angry
for the fun of it, tying them up, jumping on their backs. If
hunting is a sport, then I guess rodeo is a sport, said Kenji to
himself. But he did not seem convinced.

It wasn't bad, but it wasn't as thrilling as Henry had
anticipated. Later on, he spent more time observing the
crowd than watching the rodeo itself. The crowd had grown
restless, as if they'd been cheated. The cowboys seemed to
be having fun *for* themselves, not as if they cared about the

crowd. Kenji assumed that, as in a car race, the crowd might be excited simply because of the many dangers involved— the possibility of accidents being more exciting than the spirit of the contest. He could hardly believe this atmosphere.

The final event came. The crowd let out a tremendous roar as the two big trailers loaded with wild horses pulled into the arena. The sound of wild horses bucking inside the trailers was pronounced. They sounded as if they were going to kick the trailers apart. When the stock handlers opened the gates, ten beautiful, young, wild horses leaped out as if on cue and raced furiously around the arena floor randomly. The horses looked frightened and confused as they kicked great clouds of red dust. Rugged faced cowboys came out in teams of three to compete who could first catch, saddle and ride any one of the wild animals. The crowd was ecstatic! The horses kicked their hind legs high into the blue sky. Their muscles bunched together and then smoothed out in series after series of high front and back kicks. Their long, thick manes flowed like flames in a fire. A cowboy roped a fighting mustang, worked his way to the horse, and then twisted its smooth chestnut neck tightly in a bulldog hold with his strong arms while two other of his teammates struggled with the saddle.

Another wild horse approached just then from his blindside and smashed into the cowboy, who was holding the horse's neck, as if the two horses were working as a team. His hat shot straight up into the sky as his limp body hit the arena. The unlucky cowboy lay face down and motionless, with his arms twisted under his body. He looked very small. The accident happened in a far off corner of the arena. Kenji hoped that he was all right. No one, not even Henry, seemed affected. The spectators were high on the mega-dosage of excitement of the contests. Even the rodeo clowns had not rushed out to protect the victim from further punishment. Only two of the fallen man's team members had rushed to his side, bending over him with concern. Again, no one paid serious attention to the ambulance unobtrusively entering from the far side of the arena, a bit later. The ambulance attendants lifted the limp body of the cowboy to a stretcher and slid it to the rear of their vehicle and then slowly disappeared out of the arena. The games continued on as if nothing had happened. While the remaining cowboys struggled with the horses, a rumor ran through the crowd that the stricken cowboy had died. Kenji did not want to believe it. But, no one else in the audience seemed to mind. The games then concluded and the winners were cheered wildly, as if the crowd had seen nothing unusual and remembered even less.

Twenty-Five

After the rodeo, they all went to the Burwell Legion Club, located near the rodeo, for dinner. Inside it was very warm and semi-bright with dim lights. The room was filled with many people. All of them seemed to have attended the rodeo. They were enjoying their meals and drinks — mostly beer. Henry's group sat at a table in a corner and enjoyed lamb chops and beer. Henry paid.

After dinner, they all got into Henry's car and headed toward Roy's house again on the way back to the farm. The lowered sun was hitting their eyes directly through the opened car windows as Henry drove and a cool breeze blew in through the windows. In the West, the sky became rosy and in the East behind them it was dark. The moon had already climbed high.

By the time they arrived at Roy's house, it had become dark and the stars shone brightly in the sky above the hills. It was very peaceful. Everyone went into the house.

While Henry, Mary and Kenji sat on the comfortable sofa chairs in the living room Roy bent over, took out an old accordion from its case, and started to play. He was playing it cheerfully; moving his head and his body with the instrument very rhythmically and beating time on the floor with his foot. The music was a rollicking mixture of polka and country western. It was very quiet on the hilltop as if everything was dead except the playing of his accordion. The old man looked very happy with his music. He also seemed quite happy with his guests.

They all listened quietly to the old man's music and applauded him when he stopped playing.

Now Roy joined with them in drinking and then returned to his accordion to play more music.

Mary stood up and asked Kenji to dance. They were dancing happily from corner to corner in the spacious living room to the tunes of Roy's accordion, and then they stopped dancing and went to their chairs to drink, and Kenji urged Henry to dance with Mary, and Henry said that he didn't know how to dance.

Now Henry's group had to leave to go home and said good bye to each other. A wonderful ending to a wonderful day, Kenji thought. It wasn't until later that Kenji noticed Henry's worried expression. Maybe the trip had been too much.

Twenty-Six

The next day, Henry let Kenji take the pickup truck into town.

Kenji stepped into Denny's and sat at the counter. Inside it was cool and Lisa was reading a book. There were no customers.

"Hi, Kenji."

"Hi, Lisa."

"What a surprise visit!"

"I thought you wouldn't be working here any more."

"Why not?"

"You're the Queen."

"That has nothing to do with it," she smiled.

"Lisa, that night you looked terrific."

"Oh, thanks, Kenji. I was very glad you were there."

"I'm very glad you won."

"I didn't really expect to...and I still can't believe it."

"I thought you would. By the way, are you going to compete for the State pageant?"

"Absolutely. It's next Spring."

"I wish you luck."

"How have you been?"

"I'm doing all right."

"You have a beautiful sun tan."

Kenji was surprised that Lisa did not ask about George.

"I just stopped by for a cool drink."

"What would you like?"

"A 7-Up."

"All right."

She filled a tall glass and served him.

"Is this your day off?" she asked.

"No," he said, after he took a shp. "We just finished setting irrigation and I'm free until dinner."

"You have plenty of time, then. Do you want to go for a swim in the river?"

"That's a good idea."

"It's not that far from here. I thought you never took any day breaks."

"A tractor broke down so there's not much work to do until they have it fixed."

"How do you like farming?"

"It's hard work. I was always sleepy because I had been getting up early for the morning milking. But since the barn burnt down, I don't have to get up so early. We don't bother milking the pigs." The light banter made him feel comfortable with her.

She smiled. "Unless you're a natural-born farmer, it's not that easy."

"By the way, who is going to take care of the restaurant if we go for a swim?"

"Jane can handle it. It's been a slow day. Kenji, do you have a swim suit?"

"I have. It's in my room."

"Good."

"I'll be right back after I change," he told her. Then he thought momentarily that he wanted to shop for something for Inga. But, at the same time, it was such a hot day he would rather go swimming with Lisa.

"I'll go home too to change. I'll be back soon. I will meet you here."

"All right. What else do I have to bring with me?"

"Nothing. I'll make a simple lunch for our picnic."

"Fine," Kenji smiled.

After a quick drive home, he went into his room, quickly slipped off his jeans and put on his swim suit. He drove fast to the restaurant again to see Lisa.

Later, on the country road, Kenji and Lisa enjoyed the drive toward the Platte River where they were going to swim.

Soon, they found themselves parked in the shade of a big cottonwood tree on the grassy bank, and Lisa took out the tomato basket that had a blue bathing towel on the top. The leaves of the young and old cottonwood trees that lined the grassy banks were shining in the sun. In the far off, an old man wearing a hat was fishing. He looked very small. In the shade of big sassafras and bush, Lisa spread the bathing towel on the grass and then put the basket on it.

Next, they gladly jumped into the river and splashed warm surface water in the sun with their hands on each other's faces. The water below the surface was cool and clean and Kenji felt good. He dove deep down under the water, seeing the bottom pebbles clearly in the sunlight. Then he rose hurriedly to take a breath. Next they did it together playfully and then both came up for air at the same time.

"Race you to the shore," said Lisa. She then swam toward the grassy river bank and Kenji chased after her. He saw her wet body glisten in the sunlight when she stepped out of the water.

They sat on the beach towel and were enjoying deep fried catfish sandwiches on paper plates and lemonade that poured into paper cups from a picnic thermos bottle.

"When do you have to go back to school, Kenji?"

"This fall. I've got to register for the fall quarter. But I'm not sure. I may have to drop school if I can't get some money from my father."

"I hope you can finish school. Are you going back to Japan after you finish?"

"I'm not sure, yet."

"What about Inga? Will you marry her?"

"I don't know, yet."

"Kenji, when are you leaving for New York?"

"Next week. I'll pick up my car, go to New York and then fly back to Los Angeles."

"Will you ever come back to Grand Island?"

"I don't think so."

"How long will you stay in New York, Kenji?"

"A couple of days."

"I wish I could go to New York, too."

"Have you been New York?"

"No, never."

"This will be my first time to New York."

"I've never been anywhere outside of Nebraska."

"Nebraska is a very peaceful place."

"Kenji, if you don't mind, would you take me to New York with you?"

"No, I'm sorry. I wish I could take you with me. But the Porsche isn't my car."

"I understand."

They drank the rest of the lemonade as they were enjoying the cool breeze.

"Your hair is so soft, Kenji." She touched his dark and slightly wavy hair and she ran her slender fingers through it.

"Thank you."

"I like you, Kenji."

"I like you too." Kenji took a tall stalk of grass and put it into his mouth, holding it with his hand. He was playing with it in his mouth as he leaned back against his elbows on the towel looking out at the river and then looked at the tops of the trees gently swinging in the other side of the river.

"I want to go wherever you go, Kenji. I like you very much."

"Listen, Lisa," said Kenji as he sat up. "I also like you very much. But I can't take you anywhere."

She moved closer to him and pressed her lips to his lips, as her wet hair fell to her right cheek.

"Lisa," said Kenji, as he pushed her away, "you're very attractive but I can't..."

"I know you don't like me." She pushed her long hair back and her eyes were wet.

"I like you very much as a friend."

Then he leaned back against his elbows again on the beach towel and looked up at the white clouds moving away, thinking about George and he felt very uncomfortable.

"Lisa, George loves you."

"I'm not..." she began.

"...I'm sorry, Lisa. I wish I could take you with me but it just wouldn't work out."

"Yes, you can. You just don't want to."

"Lisa, George left home."

"When?"

"The night after the beauty contest."

"He doesn't care about me anymore, that's why."

"No," said Kenji ominously. "He left because he had a big argument with his father."

"He doesn't love me anymore. That's why he left."

"I know he loves you."

"I'm not sure."

"Yes, you are, Lisa."

"I said I'm not sure."

"All right."

"You're a coward."

"No, I am not."

"Yes, you are."

"What can I say."

"Oh, I'm sorry."

He picked up a pebble and threw it into the calm and flat

river and heard the splashing on the surface. He then looked
far up at the old man who was fishing, who seemed not to be
catching any fish.

"Isn't it peaceful here?"

"Yes, it is."

He knew that Lisa still loved George and that George
loved her. Kenji knew that Inga still loved him and he her.

"Lisa, George really loves you," he said, looking out at
nothing.

"I hate him," she responded.

They kept silent, looking out at the river.

"I'm sorry I was angry with you," she said.

"Never mind."

Kenji could see her eyes had filled with tears and he
sensed that she was still in love with George. He wrapped
her shoulders with his arm.

"Let's go back now, if you don't mind, Lisa."

"All right."

They stood up and put on their clothes over their swim
wear that was dried and packed.

Driving back to the restaurant to drop her off before
returning to the farm he thought that it was a fine picnic
except for the momentarily embarrassing situation.

Twenty-Seven

In the afternoon, Henry, Mary and John went for a drive. Kenji decided not to go and so for the first time, in more than four weeks, he had been left on the farm completely alone. Kenji felt completely at home, perhaps for the first time since he had arrived in America nearly three years ago. Los Angeles was nice, Kenji thought, but it was a world of its own. But here on the Harris farm, in the middle of America, he felt protected, insulated, assimilated. I am part of it all. Kenji wandered around the Harris house as if he had always lived there. The old Kenji who was stuck in Grand Island more than four weeks ago was as far removed from the new Kenji as Grand Island was from Tokyo. Even in his emotional pain with his family he was having a good time. He enjoyed himself, maybe for the first time in his life. He knew it would end in a week but he knew also that maybe he would be less infatuated with all this if he knew he would be working here indefinitely. He missed Inga. He wanted to be with Inga. How nice it would be being together again soon after not having seen each other for a while, he thought. That for a while seemed like a year. In a week, he would go to Jack's garage to pick up his car and leave the farm heading for New York. He would drop his car in New York and then return to Los Angeles on a flight to attend school or to drop out, whichever was called for. Henry had

161

gotten used to George's absence better than anyone now. Maybe because Kenji worked harder so that George was not missed as much as he would have been. But Mary was still very upset about George's absence. She worried about him constantly. Everytime she heard of a story of a young person being manipulated or abused, she started to cry, thinking that the same thing might happen to George. But Kenji knew that George was too smart and too strong to be taken advantage of. John missed George also, both as a brother and a friend. Kenji felt that John was just starting to realize that George was as much a friend as he was a brother to him. Even though they used to argue, there still were certain ties between them that could never be broken. In some way, John was the most affected by George's leaving. He blamed George for his loneliness now and his inability to do as much as he used to. They all wanted George back home but no one wanted him as much as John. Kenji missed George, too. Kenji especially was affected by George's leaving. His importance had risen dramatically since George left and Henry depended on Kenji more and confided in him more than when George was around. But deep inside, Kenji felt angry at himself. He felt as if the whole world were collapsing around him. An American girl was in love with him. Kenji's father hated her. And because the Porsche broke down, creating a situation where George has left home Kenji has taken his place. If he wouldn't have been here, perhaps George wouldn't have left. Kenji was not George. Kenji's conscience was not at rest.

Walking around the house, in spite of his anger, he was enjoying the atmosphere and freedom he felt. Now he sat down in a comfortable sofa with the paper and then the telephone was ringing. He debated whether or not it was right for him to answer it. He had never been alone in the house before and had never answered the Harris phone before. He decided to pick it up.

"Hello."

"Hi, Kenji!"

"Hi, George! Where are you now?"

"I am in Oklahoma City."

"What are you doing there?"

"I got stuck here. My car was stolen."

"Oh?"

"Yeah, I was on my way back from Texas, coming home."

"That's terrible."

"Kenji, I got a job on an oil platform."

"That's great."

"I wanted to see everybody before I started work in a couple of weeks. It's three months on, three months off."

"Sounds great."

"How's everything going?"

"Fine."

"Good."

"George, Lisa loves you."

"Kenji, I'm in a Greyhound Station now, and I should be back in G.I. about seven-thirty tonight. Could you tell them to pick me up at the bus terminal," said George cheerfully.

"I will. See you soon, George."

"See you later." George hung up the phone.

Kenji was suddenly relieved, not just for himself, but for the Harris family. He knew how happy they would be. No family should be separated. Henry and George would probably be going at each other again.

When the Harris's came back from their outing, Kenji rushed out of the house to meet them and told them the good news.

"Damn, I wish I knew where else that bus was stopping. I'd drive right over to the next county and meet him there. Get him home sooner." Henry was not ashamed of showing his emotion. He just wanted his son back sooner. The rest was incidental. Mary, of course, was all tears and smiles — she was making big plans for a welcome-home supper.

One of the first things Mary did, after getting the news, was to call up Lisa and invite her over for the dinner. Henry muttered something about "town girl" but Mary paid no attention to him at all. Kenji over heard Mary's side of the telephone conversation, and from the conversation, he got the idea that he was right in telling George that Lisa loved him. In fact, it sounded even better than that.

Twenty-Eight

Henry, John and Kenji left the house to pick up George. They wanted to get there earlier in case the bus arrived earlier.

On the way to the bus terminal, a white Navy car drove past them, heading in the other direction.

At the small, empty bus terminal, they sat waiting for George. The bus had not arrived.

Now, Henry stood up and paced around. He did not like to wait, anywhere, for anything, or anybody, although this might be an exception. He was still Henry Harris, bull headed.

Finally, the bus arrived. It was ten minutes late. They all went out to greet him. Three people disembarked; an old couple and then George Harris. He looked happy to be back. He grinned. The bus driver pulled out the luggage and John picked up the one that was for George.

Driving back to the house, the air was full of explanations and apologies, mostly from George. Speaking like a true son of Henry Harris, he was not apologizing for his leaving the farm but the way in which he had left and the pain he might have caused everyone by the way he did it. Anyhow, he was very glad to be back.

Henry and John filled him in on every little bit of information that he had missed in the last two weeks. John told George about the big meal their mother was planning for him when they got back home. George said he had not eaten a decent farm meal since he left. He asked his Dad about Lisa but on this topic Henry Harris was still Henry Harris. John said that mother talked to her on the phone but that she had declined a dinner invitation. George looked very unhappy. But the rest of the drive home was full of laughter and stories.

When they pulled up in front of the house, Kenji expected Mary to come running up to the car and embrace her son with a tearful hug. But she did not appear. Kenji thought she must be very busy making dinner. But when they entered the front door, there was no aroma of cooking food, no music playing, no atmosphere whatsoever. The house was very quiet.

"Mary?" called Henry. "Mary!"

There was no answer.

They walked into the living room and Henry heard sobbing coming from the upstairs. He rushed upstairs. When he entered Mike's room, where Kenji was staying, he saw that she was lying on the bed, crying, holding a picture of Mike in his Navy uniform.

"What is it? What's wrong?"

Mary continued to cry holding the picture. Finally, she stopped long enough to look Henry full in the face.

"Mike...Mike is dead from a helicopter accident on the Kittyhawk. Mike and three other boys. A Naval officer delivered the bad news just after you left."

Henry turned away from Mary and walked over to the three-masted model of a bark on the desk. He ran his fingers along the rigging. Then he walked back to the bed and sat beside Mary and hugged her gently.

Twenty-Nine

In the Grand Island Lutheran Church, a flag-draped coffin rested. Mike was at peace. The red, white and blue colors of the flag played off against the white of the church walls and the dark brown of the hardwood floor. This was one of the few funerals in Grand Island of an on-duty serviceman since the Vietnam War and so there were more members of the military and the press in attendance than might have been expected.

"We should not value someone's life by how long it was, but how they lived it...Here...Mike...he created love...his life was valuable. Let us hope his death produced something wonderful..." said the minister to the sixty-five mourners present. The eulogy was long and involved, yet well meaning. Henry seemed not to hear or react to any of it. Kenji was sitting with the family, a genuine gesture on their part, and he could not believe how sad he felt and how much he mourned someone he had never met. He only knew what Mike looked like from the photograph leaning in front of the casket and the photographs in the house. The casket was not opened, because of the fire during the accident, and Kenji would find it difficult to prove that Mike ever actually existed except for the fact that all these other people were here to mourn him. Kenji's actual mourning was the loss that Henry felt. Henry had lost his son — and his future time with Mike was not going to be in the corn fields or any place Henry hoped for.

After the service the coffin was carried to the Grand Island Veterans' Cemetery, all of the many white crosses were so bright and intensely cheerful-looking on the green lawn. The white crosses seemed almost to dance on the grass as the mourners were sitting in the folding chairs near Mike's casket.

After a brief graveside ceremony and a short prayer by the minister, the taps went on as the six sea men folded the flag that lay on Mike's coffin into a triangle shape and one of them presented that flag to his weeping mother, Mary, and saluted her. It was all a very moving scene. The only person who could not be touched by it was the person deep inside the coffin, Kenji thought.

As the casket was lowered into its grave the family came forth to throw the first bits of dirt on top of it. John was first, followed by George, Mary, Henry, Henry's parents, and then other relatives and close friends of the family. Kenji was one of those and he turned out to be the last one. Again he felt a bit strange since this was the funeral of someone he had not known even remotely. But it was all very sad. The white crosses seemed to salute the fresh new grave that belonged to the Harris family.

After the funeral, Kenji expected they would go back to the house and go on living as best they could. But, instead, Henry's family, Kenji, and Lisa all drove to Sherman Lake, forty minutes away from Grand Island, to have a beef barbecue. The broad lawns had about half dozen barbecue pits sitting here and there; several motor boats were skipping across the waves while several sail boats were sailing pleasantly in a cool breeze; a sail boat tipped over and three boys were struggling to get it right. At the other side of the lake, a newly arrived pickup truck was backing down closely to the water to release its boat into the water. A boat was pulling a water-skier who was turning in a big circle and disappeared to the other side of the lake. It was nice and cool.

It was a long picnic, full of tears and laughter and good food and beer. The inevitable remark was made several times, always accompanied by resigned sighs, that this was the kind of get-together Mike would have loved and was it not sad that it took something like this to bring them all together. The picnic was an acceptance of the fact and an attempt to live with it and deal with it on an useful level, Kenji thought. It was tradition. Kenji realized why they were having the picnic. Life must go on, and this was the best way to do it, with those you care about around you.

As the picnic continued and as the mood lightened up in direct proportion to the amount of beer and wine being consumed, Kenji noticed that this was very much a family meeting. Even though these people individually saw each other regularly, they did not meet very often as a group, it was a chance to compare notes and renew old acquaintances. Henry, after a very slow start, seemed now to be enjoying himself as much as anyone. He even managed to exchange pleasantries with Lisa, the only "town person," including Kenji, at the gathering.

Now Kenji saw George and Lisa walk off to one side and engage themselves in some deep discussion. He saw them nodding their heads in agreement, and they walked back to the others holding hands brazenly as they kept coming.

The sound and tenor of the conversation at the funeral celebration, which was what it had become, was such that George was forced to shout two or three times in order to get everyone's attention and have them quiet down. Kenji had a feeling as to what George was going to say and he wondered if this was the right time for the announcement.

"Attention everybody, please. Lisa and I have something we would like to share with you. We know that this has not been a pleasant day for any of us. So we would like to do what we can to change that. Lisa and I have decided to get married! Very soon!" There were many surprised looks.

"We're getting married because we want to. Not because we have to!" This brought out some laughs and then there was much cheering from every person — but one — at the picnic.

Everyone knew fully well who that dissenter would be. Henry turned and started to walked away from the picnic. He was not walking fast or in any particular direction. He was just walking away while the others were all congratulating the future bride and groom. He was not noticed by anyone but Kenji. He acted as if he were losing another son as he had lost Mike. Kenji imagined Henry mournfully attending the wedding ceremony at the same church where Mike's funeral was held. Kenji wanted very much to talk to Henry right now to find out what he was thinking and also to try and convince him that it was all for the best. But Henry was not ready to talk to anyone just now — including Kenji.

Thirty

To kill time before he had to head back to work in Texas, George was fixing the old tractor and Kenji was helping him.

"Hand me that box wrench by the red rag over there," George said Kenji.

Kenji handed George the tool. "George, what do you think I should do about Inga?"

"I think you should marry the girl."

"What about college? If I don't stop seeing her, my father won't send any money."

"God! Kenji, let Inga help you through school. What's wrong with that?"

"I don't want to bother her. Or maybe I don't have enough bravery to make a decision yet."

"If she loves you and you love her, there is no reason why you shouldn't help each other. It's like with me and Lisa. I hated to see her win that beauty contest, because I was being selfish. I was only thinking of myself, just like you're doing. Love means sacrifice. Lisa gave up the State pageant for me. Let Inga help you. Otherwise you don't really want her help."

"I guess you're right," said Kenji. He slowly began to feel certain about that.

"If that's the case, you can be son of your father, not

your own."

"So you think I should stand up to my father?"

"Of course. I don't mean to be cruel. But let's say you marry a Japanese woman just to please your father, then he dies. Then you will be stuck with someone you don't love and you don't even have a father to show what a fine son you were. Look at me, I made decision even though my father dislikes Lisa. So, Kenji, why not do what you want to? Because you're the one that has to live with the decision."

"But that isn't how it's done in Japan, anyway."

"Well, then, forget it."

George then got up and sat in the tractor and started the engine. It worked like new. George and Kenji smiled at each other.

"Now, we just paint it and it's like a new tractor."

"George, I will call Inga," said Kenji, and then ran into the house and picked up the phone.

"Hello."

"Hi, Inga, this is Kenji."

"Hi, Honey. Where are you now?"

"I'm still in Nebraska but I will leave here for New York next week, after I pick up the car."

"How long you will stay in New York?"

"Only a few days. Then I will fly back to L.A."

"Kenji, I miss you."

"I miss you too."

"I'm glad you called me."

"Inga, I've been thinking about us. I really love you and I want to marry you."

"When!!?"

"As soon as I graduate college. And I will get a job in the United States."

"I'm so excited. Would you please talk to my mother?"

In a moment, Mrs. Svenson came on the phone. "Hi, Kenji."

"Hi."

"I heard the news. I'm so happy for you two."

"Thanks."

"Kenji," said Inga, "I have very good news for you, too. We will talk about that after you come back."

"Good. See you soon and stay well."

"I will."

"Bye." He hung up the phone. He was so excited that he had to call his family in Japan.

When his mother answered the phone, she was in tears. Kenji had a very strange feeling.

"Kenji, your father has died."

"When?"

"This morning. He had a massive heart attack."

"When is the funeral?"

"Three days from now. Your father left some money for you in his will."

"All right."

"Kenji, your friend Takashi will talk to you."

Takashi Wakamatsu, who was working under Kenji's father, came to the phone. "Kenji?"

"Takashi, did my father mention anything about me before he died? I know he was very angry with me because of Inga."

"Yes, he was very disappointed that you wouldn't marry a Japanese girl. But that didn't mean he hated you. He was proud of you. It was just your girlfriend that upset him."

"Do you think the disappointment was what killed him?"

"I don't think so. A doctor said that probably it was *karo-shi*. There has been tremendous stress at the company lately. I think you should talk with your mother."

"Kenji," his mother said, "can you come back home to attend the funeral?"

"Yes, I will leave tomorrow."

"Good."

"Goodbye, Mom."

"Goodbye, Kenji."

Kenji hung up the phone. He was so distraught at this moment and his emotions were ready to explode. But he kept his feelings in control.

George, who had been standing nearby while Kenji was on the phone, walked up to him and asked, "What happened? You don't look too good."

"My father just died from *karo-shi*."

"What is that?"

"Death caused by overwork. It's common in Japan."

"I'm sorry."

"I have to leave for Japan immediately for the funeral."

"What about your car?"

"I forgot all about that."

"I'll tell you what. Since me and Lisa are getting married, we could deliver the car for you on our way to our honeymoon."

"It's not out of the way?"

"Nah, Lisa wants to go to some honeymoon resort called the Poconos or something. It's right near New York."

"If you really don't mind."

"No. Not at all."

"Let me call the man in Los Angeles first."

Kenji picked up the phone and made a call to Los Angeles. He explained to the man his situation and told him that he had a friend who would fulfill the delivery contract. The man was very understanding and agreed.

Thirty-One

Kenji was setting irrigation in the field, in the sticky hot early cloudy afternoon, with Henry and George and John.

"You don't have to work out here, Kenji. I don't want you to miss your flight," said Henry.

"I need to keep busy. If I don't, I will go crazy."

"I understand."

They kept working.

"These are very tall and nice, aren't they, Kenji?" said Henry proudly, pointing to the corn stalks that were high over his head.

"Yes, they are. I can't see anything from here."

"It's very difficult to know which way is which. You can get lost in the cornfield, just like in a jungle."

"Yes, very much like in a jungle."

"This is gonna be my best year ever!" said Henry, smiling. "I may make up for the last three years with this one crop."

"I know prices are going up and everyone else under-planted, but you."

"This is definitely my year! I'm gonna make out."

"Very nice," said Kenji. "I'm very happy for you and your family."

"Kenji, I was talking with John, and, for a boy, he makes a lot of sense," Henry said out of the hearing of his two

175

sons. "He doesn't know always what he's talking about but this time he has a good idea. He was telling me that if I plant soybeans here I could probably do a lot better with less effort. And that makes sense. Especially now that Mike is gone and George is gonna be leaving."

"Won't that be very expensive to start planting something else in all these fields?" asked Kenji.

"Oh, it'll cost me a bundle. But I've got to do it. I can't keep going through the cycles of the corn business. The price goes up for a year or two and then goes down for two or three years. And all the time you hoping those damn hailstorms don't hit you. I just can't take it anymore," he admitted.

"Can you afford to change?"

"With this crop, I can. I've already started ordering everything that's needed to change over to soybeans. I've actually spent money I don't even have yet. But I'll have it in about two more months as soon as the fields are brought in."

"Sounds good," said Kenji as he stopped working. He wiped the sweat from his forehead with the back of his hand.

"We may have a thunder storm today so this irrigation might be for nothing," said Henry, looking up at the sky that was slowly darkening.

"How nice if we have a cheerful shower on a hot day!"

When the sun had gone behind the clouds Kenji looked up worriedly at the darkening sky hopping that there wouldn't have any bad wind but Henry seemed not worry about the darkening sky at all.

Then, a while later, the damp south wind started to blow fiercely. The stalks bent into and then away from the wind.

Henry, this time, looked up to the dark sky with horror.

A bolt of lightening ripped across the sky, mixed with vibrating cracks of thunder.

George rushed in from his work and shouted: "Maybe this is gonna be another hail!"

"Never talk like that!" Henry shouted back. "There'll never be four hail storms in a row! It's illogical!"

It was sprinkling rain.

John and Kenji cheered, looking up at the raining sky.

Henry stood in the field like a statue staring at the sky as it became very dark as if it were night as the air chilled up like in the middle of winter.

"Dad! Dad! We gotta get out of here!" George yelled at his father, shaking Henry's shoulders.

Henry continued staring at the sky.

George stepped back and then, with all of the effort he had, gave his father a hard back hand slap, stinging his face, as the strong wind, gusting out of the northwest, drove golf-ball sized ice chunks, some even bigger.

As Kenji's compassion for his employer pushed to the limit and sudden-feeling of his anger, depression and frustration, he didn't try to cover himself as the others were hiding themselves underneath the machinery.

Then, all of a sudden, he ran away deeper into the corn-field as the hail-stones were hitting Kenji's face and arms pinging against his head, the rain-diluted blood running down from his arms and face. But he didn't feel any pain; he only felt the pain inside.

Five minutes earlier, all the men and machinery were invisible in the cornfield. Now all the men and machinery were fully visible, standing on the ground.

Looking out over the devastated corn field where all stalks were chopped down, Kenji saw John and Henry running up to him.

"Kenji, are you all right?" shouted George worriedly as he walked to him.

"I'm fine."

"Why did you do that, Kenji?" asked Henry, looking into Kenji's blood and tear-crusted face.

"I don't know. Maybe I was mourning my father."

"I don't understand," said George.

"Kenji, aren't you in pain?" asked John.

"Not at all."

"Well, I never thought you would see this damn storm," said Henry bitterly.

"It's terrible!" said Kenji, angrily kicking the ice balls with his boot.

"I know," said Henry. Unexpectedly, he smiled.

They were standing tiredly and motionlessly, much as defeated players in a game, as the dark low clouds raced to the east.

THE END